D0395450

Mirage

Annabelle Starr

EGMONT

Special thanks to:
Sarah Delmege, St John's Walworth Church of England School and Belmont Primary School

EGMONT
We bring stories to life

Published in Great Britain 2007
by Egmont UK Limited
239 Kensington High Street, London W8 6SA

Text by Sarah Delmege
Illustrations by Helen Turner

ISBN 978 1 4052 3242 5

1 3 5 7 9 10 8 6 4 2

A CIP catalogue record for this title is available
from the British Library

Typeset by Avon DataSet Ltd, Bidford on Avon, Warwickshire
Printed and bound in Great Britain by the CPI Group

'I like a bit of a mystery, so I thought it was very good'
Phoebe, age 10

'I liked the way there's stuff about modelling and make-up, cos that's what girls like'
Beth M, age 11

'Great idea – very cool! Not for boys . . .'
Louise, age 9

'I really enjoyed reading the books. They keep you on your toes and the characters are really interesting (I love the illustrations!) . . . They balance out humour and suspense'
Beth R, age 10

'Exciting and quite unpredictable. I like that the girls do the detective work'
Lauren, age 10

'All the characters are very realistic. I would definitely recommend these to a friend'
Krystyna, age 9

We want to know what *you* think about *Megastar Mysteries*! Visit:

www.mega-star.co.uk

for loads of coolissimo megastar stuff to do!

Meet the Megastar Mysteries Team!

Hi, this is me, **Rosie Parker** (otherwise known as Nosy Parker), and these are my best mates . . .

. . . **Soph** (Sophie) **McCoy** – she's a real fashionista sista – and . . .

. . . **Abs** (Abigail) **Flynn**, who's officially une grande genius.

Here's my mum, **Liz Parker**. Much to my embarrassment, her fashion and music taste is well and truly stuck in the 1980s (but despite all that I still love her dearly) . . .

and my nan, **Pam Parker**, the murder-mystery freak I mentioned on the cover. Sometimes, just sometimes, her crackpot ideas do come in handy.

Consider yourself introduced!

Rosie's Mini Megastar Phrasebook

Want to speak our lingo, but don't know your soeurs from your signorinas? No problemo! Just use my comprehensive guide . . .

-a-rama	add this ending to a word to indicate a large quantity: e.g. 'The after-show party was celeb-a-rama'
amigo	Spanish for 'friend'
au contraire, mon frère	French for 'on the contrary, my brother'
au revoir	French for 'goodbye'
barf/barfy/barfissimo	sick/sick-making/very sick-making indeed
bien sûr, ma soeur	French for 'of course, my sister'
bon	French for 'good'
bonjour	French for 'hello'
celeb	short for 'celebrity'
convo	short for 'conversation'
cringe-fest	a highly embarrassing situation
Cringeville	a place we all visit from time to time when something truly embarrassing happens to us
cringeworthy	an embarrassing person, place or thing might be described as this
daggy	Australian for 'unfashionable' or unstylish'
doco	short for 'documentary'
exactamundo	not a real foreign word, but a great way to express your agreement with someone
exactement	French for 'exactly'

excusez moi	French for 'excuse me'
fashionista	'a keen follower of fashion' – can be teamed with 'sista' for added rhyming fun
glam	short for 'glamorous'
gorge/gorgey	short for 'gorgeous': e.g. 'the lead singer of that band is gorge/gorgey'
hilarioso	not a foreign word at all, just a great way to liven up 'hilarious'
hola, señora	Spanish for 'hello, missus'
hottie	no, this is *not* short for hot water bottle – it's how you might describe an attractive-looking boy to your friends
-issimo	try adding this ending to English adjectives for extra emphasis: e.g. coolissimo, crazissimo – très funissimo, non?
je ne sais pas	French for 'I don't know'
je voudrais un beau garçon, s'il vous plaît	French for 'I would like an attractive boy, please'
journos	short for 'journalists'
les Français	French for, erm, 'the French'
Loserville	this is where losers live, particularly evil school bully Amanda Hawkins
mais	French for 'but'
marvelloso	not technically a foreign word, just a more exotic version of 'marvellous'
massivo	Italian for 'massive'
mon amie/mes amis	French for 'my friend'/'my friends'
muchos	Spanish for 'many'

non	French for 'no'
nous avons deux garçons ici	French for 'we have two boys here'
no way, José!	'that's never going to happen!'
oui	French for 'yes'
quelle horreur!	French for 'what horror!'
quelle surprise!	French for 'what a surprise!'
sacré bleu	French for 'gosh' or even 'blimey'
stupido	this is the Italian for 'stupid' – stupid!
-tastic	add this ending to any word to indicate a lot of something: e.g. 'Abs is braintastic'
très	French for 'very'
swoonsome	decidedly attractive
si, si, signor/signorina	Italian for 'yes, yes, mister/miss'
terriblement	French for 'terribly'
une grande	French for 'a big' – add the word 'genius' and you have the perfect description of Abs
Vogue	it's only the world's most influential fashion magazine, darling!
voilà	French for 'there it is'
what's the story, Rory?	'what's going on?'
what's the plan, Stan?	'which course of action do you think we should take?'
what the crusty old grandads?	'what on earth?'
zut alors!	French for 'darn it!'

Hi Megastar reader!

My name's Annabelle Starr*. I'm a fashion stylist – just like Soph's Aunt Penny – which means it's my job to help celebrities look their best at all times.

Over the years, I've worked with all sorts of big names, some of whom also have seriously big egos! Take the time I flew all the way to Japan to style a shoot for a girl band. One of the members refused to wear the designer number I'd picked out for her and insisted on sporting a dress her mum had run up from some revolting old curtains instead. The only way I could get her to take it off was to persuade her it didn't match her pet Pekinese's outfit!

Anyway, when I first started out, I never dreamt I'd write a series of books based around my crazy celebrity experiences, but that's just what I've done with Megastar Mysteries. Rosie, Soph and Abs have just the sort of adventures I wish my friends and I could have got up to when we were teenagers!

I really hope you enjoy reading the books as much as I enjoyed writing them!

Love **Annabelle**

* I'll let you in to a little secret: this isn't my real name, but in this business you can never be too careful!

Chapter One

OK, I have a confession to make. None of this would have happened if I hadn't bunked off school. Now don't get me wrong, I honestly don't make a habit of skipping school. And all I missed is lunch and then drama. It's the school play in three weeks' time, which means everyone is pretty much caught up in full rehearsal mode. That's great if you've got a good part, but I've been given the part of – wait for it – a tree swaying gently in the breeze. As you can probably guess, it doesn't exactly call for huge acting ability. That's not why

I'm bunking off, though. Seriously, I love trees and I'm not petty like that. I had decided if I was going to be a tree then I was going to be the best tree that Whitney High School had ever seen. I even went to the park and studied different types of trees – that's how dedicated I am. But last night, when I was doing my English homework, Abs' instant messaging name flashed up on my computer.

> **CutiePie:** Guess what?
> **NosyParker:** What?
> **CutiePie:** Mirage Mullins is opening Top Choonz. Tomorrow.
> **NosyParker:** You lie.
> **CutiePie:** Au contraire, mon frère. Between 1.30 p.m. and 2.30 p.m.

Mirage is HUGE. Her first single has been number one for weeks and weeks and weeks. Her video is seriously hot, too. The girl is *totally* cool. And me, Abs and Soph are her biggest fans *ever*. I've read every single article ever written about her and pretty much know everything there is to know about her, from what she has for breakfast (strawberry yoghurt and fruit, in case you were wondering) to her most embarrassing moment (when she fell over on stage, revealing her knickers to hundreds of her fans).

NosyParker: WE HAVE TO SEE HER!
CutiePie: YEP!
NosyParker: So what's the plan, Stan?
CutiePie: Meet you and Soph at the bus stop 1 p.m. Don't get caught, OK?
NosyParker: OK!

So that's how I was heading towards Top Choonz with Abs and Soph at 1.15 p.m. instead of going to drama rehearsal. Even if you hadn't heard a new music store was about to open in town, you wouldn't have been able to miss it. There were life-size pictures of Mirage in every single window and huge signs everywhere saying, 'Official Opening Today'.

The atmosphere inside the shop was buzzing. There was already a humongous queue. All around us there were girls clasping posters and CDs, chattering excitedly. There were at least seven other people who should have been at drama rehearsal (Mr Lord, our drama teacher, was so not going to be happy.) I even heard one man in a business suit nudge his friend and say, 'I'm going to get her autograph and sell it on the Internet.'

Just then, a ripple of excitement went through the queue as a sleek black limousine pulled up in front of the shop.

'This is it! This is it!' squealed Soph, hopping eagerly from one foot to another.

I was so excited I could hardly breathe. I'd been dreaming for so long about actually meeting Mirage Mullins and now it was going to happen.

For a split second there was silence as Mirage – looking totally gorgeous in a shocking-pink catsuit – slipped out of the limo, dwarfed by four burly security guards. Then, as one, the queue surged forward. The security guards shouted into their radios, while fending off the hands of grasping fans, desperate to touch their idol, all screaming, 'Mirage! Mirage! MIRAGE!!!'

'This is crazy!' I shouted above the noise to Abs and Soph.

Abs winked back at me. 'Yeah. I wouldn't have missed it for the world!' she shouted.

The three of us grinned goofily at each other. This was sooo much better than drama rehearsals. I looked at Mirage. She didn't seem scared or anything, which I would have been if I was in her shoes. She simply made her way to the front of the queue and calmly addressed the screaming crowd.

'You can all have an autograph. Just one at a time, OK?'

But no one was listening. Girls were thrusting pens and CDs at her from all sides and one woman, who looked about the same age as my mum, had thrown herself at Mirage's leg and was crying, 'I love you, Mirage. I LOVE YOU!' It was crazy. In fact I was starting to get a bit scared, especially as the girls nearest Mirage were leaping towards her as if they wanted to pull her clothes right off her body. Which is so not the way to ingratiate yourself with your idol, let me tell you.

Just as I was beginning to panic that I was going to get flattened by the crowd, three things happened at once. The security guards made a human wall around Mirage. The manager of the shop appeared and cleared his throat, before making a speech to thank Mirage for officially opening the store. And thirdly, out of the corner of my eye I spotted a familiar figure . . .

'Mum!' I hissed, ducking down behind the man in front, pulling Abs and Soph with me. The three of us watched in horror as Mum made her way into the store. She must have been on her lunch break from the council offices where she works, passed the store, heard the commotion and wandered in to see what was going on. I practically stopped breathing as she headed towards us. No way would Mum understand that the chance to meet Mirage Mullins was more important than being at school.

‘What are we going to do?’ I whispered frantically at Abs and Soph. ‘She can’t spot us. She’ll kill me!’

Abs and Soph had turned scarily pale.

‘We’ll be grounded for life,’ Abs hissed back.

I looked around wildly, desperately searching for an escape route. A few more steps and she’d be practically on top of us. Suddenly, I spotted a huge display of CDs towards the back of the store. Manically, I signalled the other two and got ready to push my way through the shrieking throng.

‘Go! Go! GO!’ I shouted and ran as if my life depended upon it. Which, knowing my mum, it pretty much did.

Out of breath, I collapsed behind the display. ‘Did she see us? Did she see us?’ I gasped at the other two.

Soph peered out.

‘I don’t think so,’ she whispered. ‘She’s looking at some CDs.’

Cautiously, I raised my head to look. Mum had a CD called *Best of the Eighties* in her hand and was

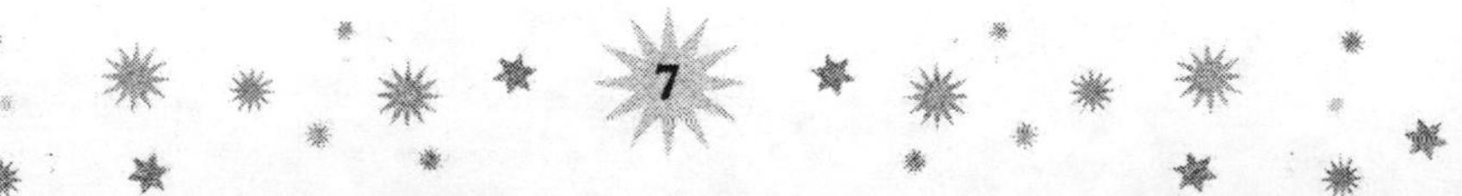

making her way towards the till. I honestly never thought the day would come when I would be grateful for Mum's totally embarrassing taste in music.

We waited until Mum had wandered out of the shop and was out of sight before getting up and sighing with relief. Then we headed back to the queue, which had thinned out considerably.

Mirage was now sitting at a table, signing CDs and posing for photos. She had a smile and a few words for every single fan, but even from where I was standing I could see the smile never quite touched her eyes. I felt for her, I really did. I've seen enough reality shows like *Newly Weds/The Osbournes/Girls Aloud Off The Record* and so forth to know how hard it must be when you're a megastar and you have to be nice to everyone all the time, even if you've got the worst toothache ever, or you've just had bad news, like your nan's been rushed into hospital, but you can't show you're upset, just in case someone thinks you're not a nice person and stops buying your records. I was determined to be extra nice to Mirage when it came to my turn and to let her know just how much her fans appreciated all her hard work.

It seemed like an age before, at long last, we were next in the queue. A few more steps and I'd be able to touch her. I could hardly stand still with excitement.

Suddenly, a huge security guard blocked our way. What the crusty old grandads!

'Sorry, girls,' he said. 'That's all Mirage has time for today.'

We stared at him in disbelief. 'But that's not fair,' gasped Soph. 'We've queued for over an hour.'

'We're her biggest fans in the world,' added Abs.

'PLEEEEEASE!' we all begged in unison.

But the security guard was completely unmoved. 'Sorry, girls,' he shrugged. 'Mirage has to leave.'

No way was I going to get this far and not meet my idol. No siree. Not me. Before the security guard could realise what was happening, I'd ducked past him.

'I'm sorry,' I gasped as I ran towards a shocked-looking Mirage. 'But I just had to meet you. I just wanted to tell you that I think you're great.'

Mirage looked nervously at the security guard, who was already bearing down on us and was, I noticed, looking pretty mad.

'I don't normally behave like this!' I gabbled. 'I just had to meet you.'

Mirage glanced at her security guard again, then quickly reached out and grabbed my hand, shaking it up and down like her life depended on it. 'I'm very glad you did,' she said, still pumping my hand up and down. 'Very glad.'

I didn't have a chance to say anything else, as right then the security guard grabbed me by the scruff of my neck, lifted me right off my feet, slung me over his shoulder and carried me out of the store. It was only after he'd literally dropped me on the pavement and walked back inside the store that I realised I was holding a scrunched-up note in my hand. Completely confused, I flattened it out, then stared at the words in disbelief.

Chapter Two

A few moments later, Abs and Soph caught up with me on the pavement.

'I can't believe you got past the bodyguard,' Abs was grinning.

'I can't believe you met Mirage Mullins,' said Sophie. 'Didn't you just love what she was wearing? I'm going to run myself up one of those catsuits this weekend.'

Trust Soph to be more interested in Mirage's clothes than anything else. Soph's going to be a famous designer when she's older. It'll be no surprise to me and Abs – she's been ripping her clothes apart and sewing them back together as long as we've known her. Soph is always the most originally dressed of all of us. While everyone else at school is wearing clothes from the high street and trying to keep up with the latest trends in magazines, Soph goes to charity shops and finds hideous dresses that probably once belonged to an old lady with five cats. Then she takes them home, pulls them apart and transforms them into totally amazing tops or skirts.

Personally, I think it's gross to wear someone else's old clothes, but Soph reckons it's perfectly hygienic – as long as you wash them a few times before wearing them.

Right now, though, I had more pressing things on my mind than Soph's dress dilemmas – LIKE THE FACT THAT I HAD A SCRUNCHED-UP NOTE FROM A FAMOUS POP STAR IN MY HAND!!!

Abs's green-eyed gaze followed mine. She looked at the note and I saw her eyebrows shoot up beneath her fringe as she read it.

'Is this for real?' she asked me, passing the note to Soph.

I nodded.

'But why would she want me to help?' I wondered. 'Mirage is a huge pop star – there must be other people she could call on. It doesn't make sense.'

'It's got to be a prank,' said Soph. 'It's probably for one of those TV shows where they play jokes on celebs or something.' She flicked her hair and pouted, peering around us, looking for hidden cameras. 'I *knew* we should have changed out of our uniforms!'

'Yeah, but on shows like that, everyone, apart from the celebrities themselves, is already in on the prank,' said Abs. 'What would be funny about winding up a bunch of schoolgirls? If it was really a prank, we'd be the ones playing it on Mirage – not the other way round.'

This is one of the reasons I love Abs – she's dead smart. But clever as she is, she still didn't have an answer for why Mirage would have written such a note in the first place.

The three of us were still discussing what on earth Mirage's note could mean when I unlocked my front door twenty minutes later.

We'd decided to head back to mine for an emergency meeting. I knew the house would be empty, as Mum was still at work and Nan always spends Tuesday afternoons in the library, picking up the latest murder-mystery books. From there, she always heads straight to Trotters – her fave café in Borehurst high street – where she has a pot of tea and an iced bun and starts the first chapter of whatever new crime novel she's borrowed in peace. Sometimes the amount of noise around our house drives her crazy. Although, I hasten to add, most of the noise doesn't come from me. Oh, no. Most of it comes from Mum's constant playing of – and singing along to – eighties tracks. Have I mentioned that Mum is in a tribute band to eighties girl band Bananarama? Mum reckons they were the Girls Aloud of their day but with more attitude and only three members. Mum totally loves being in the Banana Splits and her mission on earth is to bring the music to a more modern audience. Yeah, Mum, whatever. Honestly, I love my mum dearly, but sometimes I wish she could be a little more normal.

Anyway, Nan being at Trotters meant that we wouldn't be disturbed and could try to make sense of what had happened.

'Well, there's only one thing for it,' said Abs, no-nonsense as ever, as the three of us sat at the kitchen table, staring at the note in front of us. 'You're going to have to ring the number and find out exactly what's going on.' She reached across the table and pulled my mobile out of my jacket pocket.

'No way!' I said. 'I can't just ring it.'

Abs fixed me with her most don't-mess-with-me stare.

'Rosie, you didn't get the nickname "Nosy Parker" for nothing! You love everything to do with celebs – you live for gossip, you're always the first one to know every little thing about them. And this is your chance to talk to a celeb first hand and you're what . . . too scared?! Rosie Parker, I'm disappointed in you.'

When Abs means business, she's so scary, she's hairy. I sometimes think the girl should run for Prime Minister – a slight raising of her voice and she could get the whole country doing exactly what she wanted. Honestly, I totally mean it.

I reached for the phone, snatching it out of Abs's hand.

'Right, then, I will.'

Shaking, I dialled the number. As it rang, I put it on speaker so Abs and Soph could hear.

'Hello? Mirage?' I said as the phone was picked up at the other end.

'Oh . . . er, h-hi, *Mum*,' came Mirage's unmistakable voice. 'Nice to hear from you.'

WHAT? WHAT IS SHE TALKING ABOUT?

'Um, Mirage, it's not your, er, mother, it's Rosie . . . er, Rosie Parker – we met earlier . . .'

'Actually, Mum,' said Mirage, cutting me off, 'now's not a good time. I'm just on my way to do a radio interview.'

'Er, but it's, er . . .' I splutter.

WAY TO HOLD IT TOGETHER, ROSIE. I MEAN, SERIOUSLY!

Just then, a harsh voice spoke clearly in the background, cutting across our conversation. 'Mirage, get off the phone now! Social calls can wait. There's work to be done.'

'Y-y-yes of course, Simone,' said Mirage, 'Mum, I've got to go. I'll call you. Soon.' And the phone went dead.

Me, Abs and Soph all stared at each other.

'What. Was. That?' I said.

Before we had the chance to discuss it any further, a key turned in the front door and Mum and Nan came in. They'd obviously just bumped into each other on the doorstep.

'But why didn't you call?' Mum was saying to Nan as they walked into the kitchen. 'I'd have given you a lift home.'

'I did, Liz,' said Nan. 'About a hundred times, but it kept going to voicemail.'

'That's impossible,' said Mum, pulling her phone out of her handbag. 'I have my – oh.' She squinted at the handset. 'I forgot to turn it on this morning.'

Nan rolled her eyes to the ceiling. This was typical Mum behaviour and it drove Nan round the bend.

'Hi, girls,' said Mum. 'Good day at school?'

I could feel myself turning red. I am a terrible liar. No way would I be able to persuade Mum, or Nan for that matter, that I had been at school all day.

Fortunately, Nan had just noticed the necklace Soph was wearing. (It was made from dried pasta, all painted different colours, with glitter and sequins glued on it – let's face it, it was pretty noticeable.)

'That's an, um, interesting necklace, Sophie,' said Nan. 'You always turn up in such, er, unusual outfits.'

'Thanks, Nana Parker,' Soph beamed. 'Any time you want me to find you an unusual outfit of your own, just give me a shout.'

'The girls have to leave,' I said quickly, ushering Abs and Soph out of the kitchen, before Mum could get back on to the subject of school.

* * *

That night, I dreamt that I was on stage with Mirage, singing to hundreds of screaming fans. Suddenly, a phone started ringing really loudly and Mirage stopped mid-song to say to the audience, 'I believe we have a phone call for Rosie. Shall we put it on speaker phone so we can all hear?'

The crowd screamed their agreement. Mirage held the phone up to the microphone and the voice of Amanda Hawkins – the nastiest girl in my year – rang out loud and clear, saying, 'Rosie Parker . . . you are the worst singer EVER!'

And suddenly Mirage, together with the whole audience, started pointing and laughing at how rubbish I was and at the fact that I had ever even thought I could sing. I snatched the phone out of Mirage's hand and hung up on Amanda, shouting at her to shut up. But it just kept on ringing and ringing, while everyone kept on laughing and pointing at me.

I sat up, my heart pounding, as I realised my phone was ringing.

'M . . . wargh . . .' I said into the handset. (Well, it was the middle of the night.)

'Hello?' came a whispered voice. 'Um . . . this is Mirage . . . er, Mirage Mullins. Um, I met you earlier today at a signing – I think you tried to call me earlier.'

I sat bolt upright in bed. Let me tell you, there's nothing like a famous pop star phoning your mobile in the middle of the night to make you feel wide awake. Next time my mum is trying to get me out of bed on a Saturday morning, she should just tell me that Madonna's on the phone – that'd have me up like a shot.

'Yes! Yes, hi,' I said. 'This is Rosie Parker. I did

call you earlier, but you seemed to think I was your mum.'

'Sorry about that,' Mirage whispered back. 'I can't talk for long, but please, I need you to listen to me. I was totally desperate – otherwise I'd never have written that note.'

'Gee, thanks,' I muttered under my breath, squinting at my alarm clock. 2.45 a.m. Mirage was still talking.

'I don't know where else to turn and I'm just hoping against hope that you can help me. Like I was saying, I'm totally desperate.'

'OK, OK, I GET THE PICTURE,' I wanted to shout. 'MIRAGE IS DESPERATE. THAT'S THE ONLY REASON SHE'S CONTACTED A FOURTEEN-YEAR-OLD SCHOOLGIRL – OUT OF COMPLETE, SHEER, UTTER, TOTAL DESPERATION!'

Fortunately, instead of throwing a hissy-fit, I did the grown-up thing and tuned back in to what Mirage was saying. I listened open-mouthed as she revealed that her manager and business advisor, a woman named Simone, had blackmailed her into working for her. How? Well, basically Mirage's stepbrother, Joe, had just been arrested for stealing from the nightclub where he worked. According to Mirage, there was no way he'd have been involved in stealing any money, but he couldn't prove his innocence. Even worse, if word got out that this had happened, Mirage's career could be over. Her whole image was based on the fact that she was so clean-living and, well, basically a good girl.

For the time being, the press hadn't linked Joe with Mirage, because they had different surnames. Mirage's mum was now married to someone else, but Mirage had stayed in close contact with her stepdad and Joe because her mum was pretty rubbish at staying in touch. Simone (the evil witch) had threatened to leak the story to the press anonymously, unless Mirage stayed as her client for the rest of her career.

Listening to all this, I was in shock, I really was. I mean, I must have been – why else would I have said such mad things to Mirage?

Three things not to do when on the phone to a famous pop star who's asking for your help:

1. Interrupt her and squeal, 'I can't believe I'm talking to Mirage Mullins! On my mobile! In the middle of the night!' She probably doesn't need to hear that right now.
2. When she's telling you about her stepbrother, who has been framed for a crime he did not commit, it's probably not the best time to say, 'Oh, you're so lucky. I wish I had a brother or sister. I HATE being an only child.
3. Ask her to send you a signed photo . . .

Chapter Three

I was woken up by someone knocking on my door.

'Wake up, Rosie! Come on, wake up.' It was Nan. 'Shake a leg, there's a good girl. It's after eight, you're going to be late for school.'

I leapt out of bed, freaking out that I'd overslept, and hit the shower. It was only when I was in the shower that I remembered the night before. I couldn't believe I'd forgotten.

Running back to my room, I logged on to the Internet and typed in Simone Jones. Nothing much came up, but there was a picture of her:

sleek bobbed hair, designer clothes – basically, groomed to within an inch of her life. I downloaded the picture and pushed it into my schoolbag.

* * *

Soph took one look at my face when I came into registration and went, 'What's happened? Something's happened . . . Spill.'

Don't you just love how well your friends know you?

I opened my mouth to begin to tell her, but just then Mr Adams, our form tutor, walked into the classroom and started taking registration. Seconds later Mr Lord, our drama teacher, walked into the room without knocking, his long coat and stripy scarf billowing out behind him.

'Excuse me, Mr Adams,' he said. 'May I have a word with Rosie and Sophie please?'

'Of course,' said Mr Adams. 'Sophie? Rosie? Mr Lord would like to see you both.'

We looked at each other and groaned as we

followed Mr Lord out of the classroom.

G.R.E.A.T.

When we got outside, Mr Lord looked right at us and said, 'I heard a rumour that Mirage Mullins was at a signing in town yesterday. You girls wouldn't know anything about that, would you?'

'Um, no, Mr Lord,' we chorused, staring at the ground.

'Right, well, I just wondered, since you missed drama rehearsal yesterday.'

'Oh, no, Mr Lord,' said Soph. 'Rosie wasn't very well, you see. So I had to look after her.'

'I see,' said Mr Lord. 'Well, that makes perfect sense. I'm glad I checked.'

Me and Soph grinned at each other with relief.

Mr Lord started walking away, but then stopped as if struck by a sudden thought. He whirled round to face us again. 'Just one more thing . . .'

'Yes, Mr Lord?' we simpered, batting our eyelashes for all we were worth.

'I presume you both have a note from your parents to excuse you from drama yesterday?'

'Er . . . um . . . well, er . . . not exactly . . .' stammered Soph.

'I thought not,' said Mr Lord. 'In that case, ladies, I will see you – along with the others who missed drama yesterday – in detention after school. And I hope that will be a lesson to you all. This play should be the most consuming thing in your lives right now. I can't understand why all you young people are so impressed by celebrity. Did I ever tell you about the time I was an extra in the original series of *Dr Who*?'

'Yes, Mr Lord,' I said.

'Only about a thousand times,' Soph added under her breath.

'What was that, Miss McCoy?' Mr Lord frowned.

'Er, I could never hear it enough times?' deadpanned Soph.

Mr Lord was a Cyberman in the original series of *Doctor Who*, as he never tires of telling us.

Honestly, the amount he goes on about it, you would think he'd won an Oscar for it or something. As a result, the whole school calls him Time Lord.

'Right,' said Time Lord, running his hands through his grey hair until it stood up on end. 'Well, I was a Cyberman, you know, and as such, I rubbed shoulders daily with stars of the stage and screen, but you never caught me losing my head over them. They're just people, you know. Just people.'

'Yes, Mr Lord. You're right, Mr Lord,' we chorused, as he finally walked away.

GREAT! JUST GREAT!

That lunchtime, I filled Abs and Soph in on the events of the night before, and showed them the picture of Simone. They were as outraged and astounded as I'd been. The three of us were determined to help Mirage any way we could.

'If Simone thinks she's getting away with it then she has another thing coming,' Abs said, confidently. 'Obviously, the first thing we need to do is to speak to Mirage again.'

'Obviously,' I said, nodding wisely. 'Um, but how? Simone checks all her phone calls and messages, don't forget.'

'Simple,' said Abs. 'All we need to do is to come up with a plan.'

'Right,' I said. 'A plan. Well, that should be easy.'

'Yep,' agreed Soph. 'Easy-peasy, lemon-squeezy.'

The three of us lapsed into silence.

Hmmm . . . this coming-up-with-a-plan business was harder than I had thought. *Right. OK . . . think. I've watched so many episodes of* Murder, She Wrote *with Nan, surely some of that crime expertise must have sunk in . . . Right . . . OK . . . What would Jessica Fletcher do?* Nope . . . my mind was still a complete blank.

'There must be a brilliant solution!' I pushed back my hair in annoyance. 'Come on, Abs, you're the brainiest girl I know . . . think of something!'

'I'm trying!' frowned Abs, whipping her glasses out of her bag so she could have a closer look at the stuff I'd printed out.

'Ah, bless,' said a voice. 'Look at them, trying to learn their times tables. Sweet.' I looked up. Amanda Hawkins was towering over our table. She sat down next to me and smiled sweetly.

'Rosie, I've been wanting to ask you all day, are those new shoes?' she asked innocently. 'They're pretty.'

I gaped at her in astonishment. She smiled back at me. I *was* wearing new shoes, as it happened. Black, sequinned pumps – a bit of a change from my usual trusty trainers, but I totally loved them.

I couldn't believe it; Amanda Hawkins was actually being nice to me. *Hang on a minute – perhaps I've misjudged her all this time. Maybe there's a whole different person under that nasty exterior.* Yes, that was it! She was really very vulnerable and insecure and the reason she was so horrible was because she had put up a protective shell around herself. And I was the only one who could see beneath the nastiness and when I'd coaxed the real Amanda out into the world. The whole school would be amazed and people would call me 'The Girl Who Changed Amanda Hawkins', and . . .

'Yep,' said Amanda, her green eyes sparkling maliciously. 'Those shoes are definitely pretty. Pretty nasty.'

Oh.

I stared at her and swallowed several times. I wished I could find the ultimate retort – one that was perfect, devastating, clever and witty. But, as usual, my mind was totally blank.

'Oh, why don't you do us all a favour, Amanda – curl up and die,' said Abs.

That's what I love about Abs. Most people would be far too scared of Amanda Hawkins to say anything nasty back. But not Abs. She's not scared of anything or anyone. Abs is the kind of girl who never hesitates, stumbles or looks confused. She always knows what she wants and pretty much always gets it.

'Whatever, Specky Four-eyes,' said Amanda.

Abs spluttered with rage. It probably would

have escalated into a full-blown girl-fight, but fortunately the bell for class rang.

'Later, losers,' said Amanda Hawkins and stalked off.

'What *is* it with that girl?' asked Soph, shaking her head in bewilderment. 'D'you think she takes nasty pills every morning, or was she actually born that way?'

'Forget it, Soph,' I said, gathering up the printouts and stuffing them into my bag. 'I'll see you both in detention. Let's hope one of us has managed to come up with a cunning plan by then!'

* * *

It turned out that practically the whole cast had skipped school the previous day to try and catch a glimpse of Mirage. No wonder the queue had been so long! Me, Soph and Abs had been so busy hiding from my mum that we didn't even notice. So when we all traipsed into the main hall for detention, Time Lord announced his intention to hold a mini-rehearsal. As a tree, I didn't have anything to do in the first part of the play, so I sat at the back of the hall with Soph and Abs, supposedly helping Soph with costume design. We were actually whispering to each other about the Mirage situation. It was clear from the way Abs could hardly sit still that she'd come up with an idea. And let me just say, I will never, ever underestimate Abs again when it comes to brains. I mean, I always knew she was smart, but it turns out she's a walking genius!

***Abs** (whispering): Right, I reckon I've got this Mirage situation cracked.*
***Me** (also whispering): Tell us, then!!!*
***Abs:** Simple! Let's get her along to Dream Beauty this Saturday.*
***Soph** (whispering, of course): Dream Beauty? You mean the Dream Beauty salon where I have a part-time job?*
***Abs:** No, I mean the Dream Beauty salon in Los Angeles. Of course I mean the one where you work, idiot!*

Soph: *Oh, shut up!*

Abs: *No, you shut up!*

Soph: *No, you shut up!*

Abs: *No, you!*

Soph: *You!*

Abs: *You!*

Me: *Stop it, you two! Abs, what were you saying?*

Abs: *OK, if we can get her there on Saturday, Soph will be able to have a chat with her and find out more while she does her nails or something.*

Soph: *Only one problem. If Mirage can't even make a phone call without this Simone woman breathing down her neck, how is she going to get away from her to visit a beauty salon?*

Me: *Soph's right, Abs. We'll never be able to get Mirage there on her own.*

Abs: *Ah, but that's the beauty of my plan. We invite Simone too. It was the picture of her Rosie printed out from the Internet that gave me the idea. She's totally groomed, right?*

Me: *Right.*

Abs: *So she's bound to jump at the chance of a free bit of pampering. All Soph has to do is to ring her salon manager and persuade her to send Simone and Mirage an invitation for a day of treatments. The manager is bound to go for it – after all, looking after the biggest name in pop is great publicity for the salon. What do you reckon?*

See what I mean? The girl is a legend! Soph was already heading out the door, mobile in her hand, ready to call the salon manager.

'I'm on it!' she mouthed as she went.

'Genius!' I grinned at Abs. She gave a casual shrug of her shoulders, but I could tell she was pretty pleased with herself.

A few minutes later, Soph came bounding back into the room, her brown pigtails bouncing.

'We're on,' she grinned. 'I spoke to the manager and she thought it was a brilliant idea. She's faxing an invite to Mirage and Simone's office now. Oh, and I booked you both in for a manicure on Saturday. I thought it might be an idea if we were all there together. What do you think?'

Me and Abs grinned at each other, 'Can't wait!'

Chapter Four

On Saturday morning, me and Abs walked into Dream Beauty. Mrs Blessing, the manager, was obviously over-excited at the prospect of having a real-life celebrity in her salon, judging from the way she greeted us.

'Hello, girls,' she beamed. 'Welcome to Dream Beauty, where our motto is . . .'

'No, no, don't tell me,' interrupted Abs. 'Let me guess. Um. Is it: "Where all your beauty dreams really do come true . . ."?'

'No,' said Mrs Blessing.

'OK,' said Abs, screwing up her face with concentration. 'Well, is it . . . er . . . Let me think. I've got it! Is it: "You dream, we beautify!"?'

'No, it's not,' snapped Mrs Blessing, looking annoyed.

'Hmmm. Is it . . .'

'It's: "Dream Beauty, where we'll make you feel a million dollars",' snapped Mrs Blessing, cutting Abs short.

'Oh,' said Abs. 'Well . . . um . . . that's good too.' She leant over to me and whispered, 'What a totally rubbish motto. Mine were much better.'

Unfortunately, her whisper was rather loud and Mrs Blessing spun round, giving us a rather beady look. Luckily, at that moment, the door to the salon opened and Simone, already looking totally and utterly immaculate, swept in. Two steps behind her was Mirage, accompanied by a huge bodyguard (not the same one who'd picked me up by the scruff of my neck, I was relieved to see). Mrs Blessing went rushing over to greet them.

I couldn't help but stare at Mirage, who was

looking totally gorgeous with all her long blonde hair pulled into a side ponytail. (I wish my hair would do the same as hers – unfortunately my hair normally resembles a bird's nest. Actually, even describing it as a bird's nest is probably an insult to birds everywhere. Basically, it's an unruly mop.) She was wearing a simple black tank top and jeans, with jewelled flip-flops, and looked totally amazing.

Abs nudged me hard in the ribs. 'Get up!' she hissed.

Me, Soph and Abs had already agreed that me and Abs would act like normal fans who are stunned to see their pop idol walk into the salon where they have come for a manicure. I jumped to my feet and rushed over to Mirage.

'H-h-hello. It's great to meet you,' I gabbled. 'My name's Rosie. Rosie Parker. I'm a huge fan.'

Mirage looked completely gobsmacked to see me there. I glanced at Simone. She looked completely expressionless, but I could see from the flicker of her eyelashes that she was giving us the once-over. Reaching out to shake Mirage's hand, I managed to position myself so my back was to Simone.

'It's OK, we've got a plan,' I mouthed. 'Trust me.' Out loud, I said, 'And this is my really good friend Abs. She totally loves your music too.' Abs came rushing over.

'I can't believe it – Mirage Mullins in our local beauty salon,' she gushed, winking at Mirage. 'Who'd have thought it? Just wait till the girls at school hear about this. They'll never believe it. Can we get a picture of you with us later? And your autograph? I'm so excited, I think I might actually wet myself!'

I frowned at Abs, trying to let her know by the power of telepathy that she might *possibly* be ever-so-slightly overdoing it.

Mirage stared from one of us to the other. 'Um, it's nice to meet you both,' she said. 'This is my manager, Simone.'

'Nice to meet you, Simone,' I smiled. Simone looked down her nose at me, and her mouth extended by three millimetres, which I'm guessing was her equivalent of a smile. Then she turned to Mirage.

'Mirage,' she said. 'I'd like some tea.'

'I'll go and sort it out,' said Mirage, rushing off to find Mrs Blessing, while Simone coolly sank into a chair and flicked through a magazine. Me and Abs gaped at each other. Honestly, it was as though Simone was the hugely successful pop star and Mirage was a complete nobody.

Mirage reappeared. 'It's on its way, Simone,' she said nervously. Simone nodded without even bothering to look at Mirage. I shook my head in disbelief. Who did she think she was? Well, Miss Snooty was going to talk to me, whether she liked it or not.

'How lucky you must feel to be managing someone as beautiful and as talented as Mirage,' I gushed.

'Indeed.' Simone gave a wintry smile and, after a moment's hesitation, reached out and placed her hand on Mirage's shoulder. I saw Mirage try not to flinch. I wasn't surprised – being touched by Simone must have been like being touched by the Ice Queen. Seriously yucky!

Mrs Blessing came bustling over with a pot of tea and a plate of cream cakes, which she carefully placed in front of Simone, who stared at the plate as if she had just been presented with a dead rat.

'Rude is not the word!' Abs whispered in my ear.

'Do help yourself to a cake,' said Mrs Blessing, picking up the plate and holding it out to Simone.

'I don't think so,' said Simone, flinching away from the plate as if the cream particles might actually be floating through the air and invading her body. She stood up and brushed an imaginary crumb off her skirt. 'Let's get on with this, shall we?'

'Of course,' said Mrs Blessing. 'Simone, if you'd like to come this way for your facial . . . Mirage, you're booked in for a manicure. Sophie!' she called.

Soph appeared from a side room. 'Yes, Mrs Blessing?'

'Your client is here,' said Mrs Blessing, leading Simone into one of the consulting rooms.

'It's a pleasure to meet you, Mirage,' Soph said with a professional smile. 'Would you like to come with me, please?' She turned to me and Abs and winked. 'I believe you two ladies are also booked in for a manicure. If you'd like to come with me, I'll make sure you're looked after while you wait.'

The three of us followed Soph to the nail bar over by the window of the salon.

'See – told you my plan would work!' grinned Abs.

'Not quite,' I hissed.

'What do you mean?' asked Abs.

'How do we get rid of him?!' I nodded grimly over her shoulder. Abs glanced behind her to see the burly bodyguard standing there, watching us closely. Abs raised her eyebrows. 'Not a problem,' she said.

She cleared her throat loudly. 'So, Mirage,' she said, 'me and Rosie here are your biggest fans in the world. Tell us everything. And I mean

everything . . . What's your favourite colour?'

Mirage looked slightly startled. 'Um, blue,' she said.

'Right, right. Interesting,' said Abs, nodding her head as if Mirage had made the most profound statement ever. 'What was your worst subject at school?'

'Maths,' said an obviously bemused Mirage.

'Ooh, me too,' said Abs. 'What a coincidence! You know, I always thought we'd have loads in common if we ever met. I always thought we could be best friends. I'm always saying that, aren't I Rosie?'

I stared at Abs in disbelief. She'd never said any such thing. Seriously, Abs is far too sensible to say anything like that. Honestly, she was more likely to say she was becoming the sixth member of Girls Aloud.

'What about your best subject?' Abs went on. 'No, don't tell me . . . music!'

I looked over at the minder, who rolled his eyes at the ceiling. 'Is she always like this?' he asked.

'No, nev–' I started to say, when Abs kicked me hard. 'Ow . . . I mean, yes, yes she is. She can't help herself. Seriously, it's like a disease.'

'Whatever,' the bodyguard sighed. 'I've got better things to do with my time than listen to your little friend go on and on.'

And with that he wandered off to talk to the extremely pretty receptionist.

'Thought we'd never get rid of him,' beamed Abs. 'Sorry about that,' she said to Mirage. 'I'm not a crazed fan, honestly – it's just, if the four of us are going to be able to talk properly, we can't do it with one of your minders earwigging. Rosie filled us in on what's going on and we decided we had to get you here so we could work out a way to help you. I'm Abs, and this is Soph.'

Mirage beamed at me. 'That's inspired. I didn't know what to think when I walked in and saw you standing there. It was all I could do not to let on to Simone that I knew you!'

'I'll tell you what,' said Soph. 'I'd have known the minute I laid eyes on Simone that she was dodgy.' She narrowed her eyes wisely. 'You can totally tell by her outfit.'

'What?' said Mirage, glancing over at the bouncer to check he was still out of earshot. 'You mean you can tell what someone is like by what they're wearing?'

'Oh, absolutely,' confirmed Soph, the tip of her tongue sticking out of the corner of her mouth with concentration, as she painstakingly applied varnish to Mirage's nails.

'OK, so, what can you tell from Simone's outfit?' asked Mirage.

This is something Soph's always done – checked out people's clothes and listed them in her head as if they were on a fashion page.

'OK. Well, I can tell by her suit – which is totally designer – that she's confident about her body and that she's totally obsessed about the way she looks. Her shoes are Fabconis.'

Me and Abs stared at her blankly.

'Basically, they cost a minimum of three hundred pounds – they could even be more than a thousand.'

'Nooo!' me and Abs chorused.

Soph grinned at us before continuing. 'That means she likes having a LOT of money. Her handbag is expensive and carefully chosen to show off how much money she has. And she had a full-on face of make-up, even though she has come for a facial, which means she wears make-up as a mask and doesn't want anyone to see the real her. She kept her sunglasses on inside, which means she's definitely got something to hide . . .' She paused and grinned at Mirage. 'How am I doing so far?'

Mirage stared at her open-mouthed. 'You got all that just from an outfit?'

'Yup,' Soph winked. 'It's a talent. Clothes tell you everything you need to know about a person.'

'Wow!' said Mirage.

After that Mirage relaxed, especially when Abs did a really good imitation of Simone looking at the cake as if it was about to mug her and we all started laughing hysterically – until the minder walked over and asked what was so funny and we had to pretend we were laughing at a joke on the radio.

I suddenly felt like I was in a movie. I wasn't Rosie Parker, ordinary schoolgirl, daughter of Liz Parker (slightly nutty eighties music fan) and granddaughter of Pam Parker (murder-mystery-mad old lady). This was Rosie Parker, sophisticated friend to the stars, chatting, over a manicure, to a famous pop star. If Amanda Hawkins could see me now, she wouldn't believe it.

I looked up and saw Mirage staring at herself in the mirror. Suddenly all the animation seeped out of her face. She met my eye in the mirror and I felt a sudden pang of outrage.

'Tell us how we can help you, Mirage,' I said.

She smiled at me sadly. 'OK, you need to contact my stepdad, Mike Matthews. He lives at forty-nine Willow Road, in Fleetwich.'

'Forty-nine,' nodded Soph. 'Got it.'

'Fleetwich; I know it,' said Abs. 'My nan lives there. It's only a bus-ride away.'

'Cool. Tell him I sent you to help Joe. You'll

meet him, too. He's staying there until the court case. If you need to get any messages to me, Mike will pass them on.'

'But I thought Simone checked all your messages,' I said.

'She does,' Mirage sighed. 'I'm only allowed to talk to Mike on speakerphone in Simone's presence. But what Simone doesn't know is that, when Mum and Mike were married, when me and Joe were kids, we used to have a code so Mum would never know what we were going on about. Joe's filled Mike in on the code, so Simone thinks we're talking about one thing, but actually we're talking about something completely different.'

'That's brilliant!' gasped Abs.

Soph cleared her throat warningly. Simone had reappeared and was tapping her foot impatiently, looking daggers at us. Seriously, it's lucky that looks can't actually kill, or else me, Abs and Soph would all be goners. I'm not kidding.

'Um, anyway, what's Britney Spears like?' Abs improvised quickly as Mirage got up from the table.

When the minder opened the door, flashbulbs went off. Mrs Blessing had obviously tipped off the press about her famous client. As Mirage stepped outside, we could hear journalists shouting questions.

'Mirage! Tell us, what's your favourite colour?'

'Have you ever met Britney?'

'Honestly,' said Abs loudly, 'can't they think of anything more original? Seriously, I could think of at least ten more interesting questions than that off the top of my head!'

The minder stared at her as if she was totally crazy, before shaking his head and closing the door behind them.

Chapter Five

A short bus journey later, we were standing outside 49 Willow Road. Soph had managed to persuade Mrs Blessing to let her leave work early so she could come with us. Still on a high from having such a close brush with fame, Mrs Blessing was only too happy to let her go. Luckily, she didn't even notice that neither me nor Abs had had manicures.

'Right,' I said nervously, staring at the house. 'What's the plan?'

'Plan?' asked Abs. 'To ring the doorbell and ask for Mike, obviously.'

'But shouldn't we work out what we're going to say?' I asked.

Abs wasn't listening; she was already marching up the driveway, her dark bob bouncing with determination. Me and Soph glanced at each other then scuttled to catch up with her, just as she was ringing the doorbell.

A few moments later, a man around my mum's age opened the door. He looked awful, all pale and miserable, and – as a horrified Soph pointed out later – he was wearing seriously terrible clothes. His face was taut and his shoulders were all hunched up. He looked at us suspiciously. 'Yes?' he said.

'Are you Mike Matthews?' asked Abs.

'When will you journalists get it into your heads that my son and I have got nothing to say to you?' the man snarled, trying to shut the door.

Journalists? He thought we were old enough to be journalists. How cool was that? I couldn't help beaming at him. Ooh, I could just imagine myself as a journalist. I'd spend all my time jetting off around the world to glamorous locations to interview famous people, and I would manage to ask so many insightful yet sympathetic questions that celeb after celeb would totally open up to me, revealing things about themselves that they'd never told a living soul before, and it wouldn't be long before they'd refuse to be interviewed by anyone else, and I'd be the most sought-after journalist ever. I'd probably be given my own talk show, and Hollywood studios would fight over the film rights to my life story . . .

Abs's hand shot out, stopping the door from closing and snapping me back to reality.

'Mr Matthews – Mike,' she said, still holding on to the door, 'I promise you we're not journalists. Actually, we're still at school. Mirage sent us.'

'I don't know any Mirage,' said the man, pushing against the door. 'How many times do I have to tell you people to go away? Please, just leave me and my son alone.'

'No, honestly Mike, it's true,' I said, stepping forward. 'I met Mirage at a signing and she asked us to help her. She was the one who said to contact you. Look . . .' I fumbled in my bag, pulling out my mobile phone. I quickly scrolled through to 'received calls' before holding it up to him. 'Here's Mirage's phone number. Look, you can see she called me. Seriously, you can trust us – we're here to help.'

Mike peered at the phone. Drawing back, he hesitated for a moment, then shook his head. 'No, I'm sorry,' he said. 'Please just leave.' And he made to shut the door again.

'Wait!' pleaded Abs. 'We know about the code you use to fool Simone – the one that Joe and Mirage made up when they were kids. How would we know that if we weren't who we said we were?'

Mike stared at us all for a moment. Then, sighing, he held the door open. 'Come in,' he said.

We followed him down the hallway and into the lounge.

'Please, sit down,' he said, nodding towards a battered old leather sofa. Me, Abs and Soph sat.

'I'm sorry for being so harsh with you,' said

Mike, sitting opposite us on a matching chair. The chair let out a creak that sounded an awful lot like a fart. I could see Soph out of the corner of my eye trying to smother her giggles. I nudged her, hard. 'I just had to be sure you were telling the truth. For all I knew Simone could have sent you.'

'That witch? No *way*,' Abs said with feeling.

There was a tense silence.

'Um, this is a lovely room, Mike,' I said, looking around me, desperately trying to lighten the atmosphere. I patted the sofa. 'My mum would love a sofa like this, but my grandmother, who lives with us, won't let her get one. She said the last time she sat on a leather sofa was at the library. She decided to have a bit of a sit-down, but she slid right off the shiny leather and ended up skidding across the floor. She landed on the lap of a very surprised librarian!' I was babbling. I knew I was, but I couldn't seem to help myself.

'You know the worst thing about all of this,' Mike said, as if I hadn't spoken. Well, I couldn't blame him really.

'Your clothes?' Soph joked under her breath. I squeezed her hand hard to get her to shut up. 'Ow! Stab me next time, why don't you?' she hissed at me.

Mike looked at us, his eyes full of misery. 'It's that it's so hard to trust anyone any more.'

Me, Abs and Soph looked at each other helplessly. I totally wished I could think of something wise and comforting to say, but my mind was a complete and utter blank. The next minute, the front door slammed.

'I'm home, Dad,' shouted a voice. 'I got some stuff for dinner, so I hope you're hung– Oh, I didn't realise we had visitors.'

I looked up and gulped. A total vision of gorgeousness had just walked into the room – tall and thin, with dark floppy hair and striking blue eyes. Mike stood up.

'This is my son, Joe,' he said. 'And these are friends of Mirage's. They're here to help. I'm sorry, I don't actually know your names.'

Soph jumped up. 'I'm Sophie,' she said,

fluttering her eyelashes, 'But everyone calls me Soph. This is Rosie and this is Abs. We're here to help in any way we can.'

Joe rubbed his hands over his face as if he was completely exhausted, as he sat down on the arm of his dad's chair. 'It's nice to meet you. I really don't want to be rude, but I don't see how you can possibly help.'

'Not unless you know how to get hold of the CCTV footage that's missing,' said Mike.

'What missing CCTV footage?' asked Abs.

'Well,' Mike started to explain, 'the money that went missing –'

'The money I've been accused of stealing,' Joe interjected.

'Yes,' said Mike, placing his hand comfortingly on Joe's shoulder. 'Well, it was kept in a safe in the main office. The keys to the safe were kept in the right-hand drawer of the desk in the office.'

'I know, I know. Not the best hiding place,' said Joe. 'But we're a tight-knit team at the club, and we thought everyone on the staff was trustworthy.'

He shrugged. 'Looks like we were wrong.'

'But there was a CCTV camera above the safe which showed anyone coming into the office and, more importantly, exactly what they were taking out of the safe,' Mike said.

'But that's brilliant,' I said excitedly. 'It'll show exactly who the thief is.'

'Only one problem,' said Mike. 'It's missing.'

'So how come they accused you, Joe?' asked Abs.

'I was the last person to be seen going into the office. The police investigated, but once they heard I was the last one there, they stopped looking for anyone else and arrested me.' Joe looked really upset.

'There's one thing I still don't understand,' I said. 'How did Simone get wind of you being arrested?'

'Didn't I say?' Joe smiled bitterly. 'She owns the club. That's how she got to be Mirage's manager. She saw Mirage singing karaoke one night and signed her up on the spot.'

I could have sworn Joe's blue eyes welled up as he looked at us. 'I didn't touch the money. I'd never do anything like that. And now Simone is blackmailing Mirage over it. I know if I could just get into the club I'd be able to find something to prove my innocence, but Simone's banned me and Dad from going anywhere near it!' His voice cracked and he hid his face in his hands.

'It's OK, Joe,' I said. 'We're on your side. We promised Mirage that we'd help and we will.'

If only I had a clue how, I added, silently. How on earth were we going to help Mirage and Joe out of this mess? How? HOW?! HOOOOOOOOOOO-WWWWWWW?!!! I started reciting the alphabet backwards in my head in a French accent to stop my panic from showing.

Abs got to her feet, signalling to me and Soph to do the same. 'Well, it sounds like we have to work out a way to get into that club,' she said. I looked at her in admiration. Nothing ever throws Abs; she cuts through problems, straight to the solution, as easily as a knife through butter. She's always calm under pressure, unlike me. I'd got as far as 'T' with the alphabet-backwards-with-a-French-accent thing in my head, and the panic I was feeling inside wasn't showing any sign of disappearing.

'We'll leave you to it,' Abs said, shaking Joe and Mike by the hand. 'Thank you for being so honest with us. If you can leave it with us, we'll get back to you with some ideas on what to do next.'

'I'll see you out,' said Mike.

Joe stood up, 'I'm still not sure how you can help,' he said. 'But it means a lot that you're willing to try.'

Mike ushered us out into the hallway.

'You know, Joe has been amazing during all of this,' he confided, as he scribbled something down on a piece of paper. 'Mirage has pleaded and pleaded with him not to listen to Simone's blackmail and to let her do her worst, but Joe's made up his mind that Mirage's career shouldn't be wrecked over this. He's even told her that he'll go to prison if it means her dreams of being a star come true. The truth is that Mirage has spent her life with a mother who has moved from boyfriend to boyfriend with absolutely no stability and no real home. Now she really has a chance to do something for herself and Joe's determined he isn't going to be the one to stop it from happening. It shows how much Mirage loves him that she's reached out to you three schoolgirls in the desperate hope you might be able to help.'

Honestly, I thought – totally forgetting that I'd been caught up in practically a full-blown panic attack minutes earlier – *what is it with this Mirage-having-to-have-been-totally-desperate-to-have-contacted-me thing? Get over it, people!*

Abs reached out and laid a hand on his arm. 'Don't worry, Mr Matthews,' she said. 'We'll find a way through this, I promise.'

'Thanks,' he said. 'Here's our phone number, in case you should need it.' He pressed the piece of paper into Abs' hand.

Once outside, the three of us stopped and looked at each other.

'Wow!' I said.

'I know!' agreed Abs.

'Yes, indeedy!' said Soph. 'Could Joe look any more like a male model?!'

Me and Abs stared at her in disbelief.

'Er, Soph?' I said. 'I meant wow as in "Wow! What that poor family are going through . . ."'

'Well, *duh*!' said Soph, 'But come on – he was seriously hot. You two must have been thinking the exact same thing. I mean, couldn't you just see him on the pages of a fashion mag?'

'He was good-looking,' I agreed. 'But at least eighteen, so way too old for you.'

'Good-looking? Good-looking?!' Soph spluttered. 'That's like saying Paris Hilton is a little bit rich. Honestly, Rosie – you're hopeless.'

I rolled my eyes at Abs. Luckily, Soph was too busy trying to find words to describe the vision that was Joe to notice.

'He isn't just handsome – his face is filled with kindness, intelligence and humour, too,' she sighed. 'Even his voice is nice: deep and understanding.'

'Whatever, Soph,' said Abs. 'But seriously, we need to work out what our next move is. We have to get into that club. And we have to work out how . . .'

Chapter Six

When I came down to the kitchen the next morning, Mum was tidying up the breakfast things with one hand while drinking tea from a mug that read, 'You don't need to be mad to be in a tribute band . . . but it helps.'

'Morning, sleepyhead,' she smiled, in a way that, to someone who had hardly got any sleep cos they'd spent the night stressing about how they were going to help a pop star in trouble, might be slightly irritating. 'Sleep well?' she asked.

I shrugged grumpily. I'm seriously not a

morning person. Mum, on the other hand, most definitely is. She started singing along to the radio at the top of her lungs.

'Seriously, Mum, you have *way* too much energy for this time in the morning.'

'Oh, honey, how can I not be in a good mood? The sun's shining and there's a Wham! song on the radio,' she smiled. She carried on singing as she swung a dirty tea towel round her head along to the music before flinging it into the washing machine.

'Keep it down in there,' shouted Nan from the living room. 'I'm trying to watch *Diagnosis Murder*!'

Nan is always grumbly when anyone makes the slightest bit of noise during one of her favourite shows. One time I sneezed halfway through Hercule Poirot's summing-up at the end of a particularly complicated case and Nan didn't speak to me for half an hour! I'm not joking!

I rolled my eyes, grabbed a bowl and stomped over to the cupboard to get myself some cereal. Plonking myself down at the kitchen table, I pulled the Sunday paper towards me. A picture of Mirage leaving Dream Beauty stared up at me. I sighed. How on earth were we going to get into the club? And even if by some miracle we managed that – which seemed highly unlikely, seeing that we were only fourteen – how were we going to sneak into the office without anyone noticing, so we could look for clues?

'Rosie, are you OK?' said Mum.

Suddenly, I realised I had been absent-mindedly drumming so hard with a pencil on the kitchen table I was in danger of making a dent.

'I'm absolutely fine,' I said, with an over-bright smile. 'Why wouldn't I be?'

Mum stared at me closely. I suddenly felt really paranoid – as though my secret was so huge, I was somehow giving it away. As though Mum must be able to see it floating above my head in huge bubble captions, like you get on photo stories in magazines.

'Is that the time?' I asked, making a great show out of looking at my watch. 'I'd better get myself ready. Time – um, I mean, *Mr* Lord's called an emergency rehearsal of the school play. Apparently we're totally behind schedule.'

* * *

Two hours later, I was halfway through the scene where I was a tree. A tree that didn't even have a speaking part, I might add. A tree that was totally in the background. But Time Lord obviously didn't see it that way. In fact, from the way he was acting, you'd think I was playing Juliet or something.

'That, Miss Parker,' he snapped, 'was *awful*! I've seen patients on trolleys in *ER* with more animation than you.'

As you can probably tell, Time Lord was NOT HAPPY!

'I'm trying my best, Mr Lord, honestly,' I groaned, rubbing my aching arms. Seriously, holding your arms in the air for half an hour is NOT easy. 'It's quite hard to look tree-like.'

'Hard?' Time Lord's eyes glittered. 'Hard? You

don't know the meaning of hard. You should try wearing a Cyberman's outfit for nine hours at a time on a boiling hot summer's day – then you might *begin* to understand the concept of hard!'

Amanda Hawkins, who of course had the lead in the play, stepped forward. 'I agree with you, Mr Lord. I have to say, I thought Rosie was looking quite *wooden* in that last scene.' She sniggered loudly.

OH, HA-DE-HA-DE-HA! SOMEONE CALL AN AMBULANCE; I MIGHT SPLIT MY SIDES LAUGHING!

'Exactly, Amanda,' Time Lord said.

'In fact,' she went on, smiling spitefully at me, 'if I were you, Mr Lord, I'd give up . . . I think you're *barking up the wrong tree* with your casting of Rosie in this play.'

SERIOUSLY, THAT GIRL SHOULD HAVE A CAREER AS A COMEDIAN.

'Now, now, Amanda,' said Mr Lord. 'Rosie, I really want you to get into the mindset of being a tree.' He stretched out his arms. 'Feel the leaves on your branches unfurling . . . Feel the breeze running through them . . . Let your imagination take hold, fire you, inspire you . . . Let it carry you away to a forest . . . I want you to go to the back of the hall and practise. Next time I see you back on this stage I don't want to see *you*, I want to see a tree, do you hear me?!'

I stomped off to the back of the hall. As the drama rehearsal went on around me, I sat on a stool, trying to hold my arms out in a tree-like manner, while my mind still fretted on the subject of Mirage.

Soph came bounding over, her arms full of costumes.

'Phewee, tiger! Am I exhausted?!' she exclaimed, dumping the costumes on the stool next to me. 'I stayed up all last night making these.'

'You made all of these last night?' I asked incredulously as I reached for one of the costumes. A piece of ribbon fell off on to the floor.

'Yeah, I couldn't sleep,' she sighed. 'Too busy

worrying about the Mirage situation and how we're going to get into this club.'

I stared at Soph, impressed. Perhaps this play would be it for her. Maybe a fashion buyer would be sitting in the audience and would spot Soph's potential. And she'd ask Soph to run up a few samples for her. And a famous film star would wear one of her creations to a red-carpet event and there'd be a mad rush for them and Soph would become a totally hot designer. And me and Abs would get to wear her clothes for free, cos we knew her way back when she was nobody, and cos we'd always believed in her.

Abs, who had wandered over, picked up one of the costumes by the arm. As the sleeve fell off, she rolled her eyes. OK, make that *nearly* always believed in her.

'Um, Soph?' said Abs, picking up another costume, 'do you realise this one is unravelling at the back?'

'OK,' shrugged Soph, 'so I don't do my best work when I haven't slept.' She glanced at me.

'You're very quiet today, Rosie.'

'As if anyone can get a word in with you around, Miss Big Mouth,' I smiled.

'Seriously, Rosie, what's up?' Abs asked.

'I just can't stop thinking about Mirage,' I sighed. 'I just can't see how we're going to help her.'

'I know, I know,' Abs nodded, sympathetically. 'But we'll come up with something, Rosie. I know we will.' She patted my arm quickly, about to head off to the stage to rehearse her scene. Abs had managed to land the part of Old Woman in Crowd. Not the most exciting role in the world ever, but hey, at least it's a step up from a tree. 'Leave it with me, I'll think of something.'

True to her word, half an hour later, she was back, grinning from ear to ear.

'I've got it!' she said, practically dancing up and down on the spot. 'I just heard Amanda Hawkins boasting that she'd got tickets to a secret Mirage Mullins gig on Wednesday night. And guess where this secret gig is!'

'The club?' I said.

'Uh-huh,' nodded Abs, excitedly. 'Problem of getting into the club solved.'

'Not exactly,' Soph said. 'I hate to break it to you, but we haven't got tickets to the gig.'

'Where there's a will, there's a way,' smiled Abs, tapping her nose. 'Leave it with me – I'll think of something!'

* * *

That evening, I was at home in my room, still trying to work out how the crusty old grandads to look more like a tree. Let's face it, no way was Time Lord getting off my back until I had it down. Anyway, I was trying to work out the best way to make my hands resemble leaves when I got instant messaged by Abs.

CutiePie: What are you doing on Wednesday night?
NosyParker: Hmmm, let me think . . . Wednesday. A school night. Tricky . . .

Oh, yes, that's right. Absolutely nothing.
CutiePie: Funny.
NosyParker: I know. It's a gift.
CutiePie: Anyway, as I was trying to tell you, we're on for the secret gig at the club.
NosyParker: No way!
CutiePie: Way, way, waaaaaaaaaay!

I could see Soph was online so involved her in the conversation:

NosyParker: Guess what?
FashionPolice: What?
NosyParker: Abs has only gone and sorted us out tickets for the secret gig on Wed!!!
FashionPolice: Nooooooooooo!!! How?
CutiePie: Dur! I rang Mike.
FashionPolice: Ooh, did you speak to the lovely Joe?
NosyParker: Focus, Sophie, focus!!!

FashionPolice: Sorry.

CutiePie: As I was saying, I spoke to Mike and he spoke to Mirage – using their code, of course – and she's sending tickets to you, Soph, at Dream Beauty. That way it looks like they're just a thank you for the free treatments yesterday – which means Simone won't get suspicious.

NosyParker: That's genius, Abs! How do you do it?

CutiePie: Oh, stop – you'll make me blush! One more thing – she's also sending backstage passes, which means . . .

NosyParker: We can get to the office to look for clues!

CutiePie: Yes indeedy!

FashionPolice: Why don't you both stay at mine? Mum and Dad are going to a party that night.

NosyParker: Sounds like a plan.

I would have talked for longer, but Mum yelled at me to get offline. She was expecting a call about a booking for the Banana Splits. Sometimes I really wish we had broadband. And that Mum could be a little more normal instead of being completely fixated on some out-of-date band that no one under the age of thirty has ever heard of (and let's face it, what does anyone over that age know about music?). Don't get me wrong, it's not that I don't love her. She just doesn't get that it's totally embarrassing having your mum dress up in dungarees, checked shirts and clumpy boots. I mean, would it kill her to wear a nice pair of jeans and a sweater once in a while, like all my friends' mums?

Chapter Seven

On Wednesday night, we were getting ready in Soph's bedroom.

'I feel so nervous, I could actually throw up all over the carpet,' I said. I wasn't joking. I honestly felt like I could barf up the contents of my stomach at any moment.

'Ha, ha!' shrieked Soph, laughing helplessly. 'Do you remember that time when we were at Trotters and we dared you to eat five doughnuts in a row? And you did? But then you felt really sick and ended up throwing up in that old lady's shopping bag?'

She laughed so hard, she completely missed her mouth with her lip-gloss wand and it went up her nose instead.

'Yes,' I said. 'Funnily enough, I do – thanks for the reminder, though. Way to make me feel better, Soph. But seriously, what happens if we get caught?'

'We won't,' said Abs, brushing her dark hair till it shone. 'And even if we did, we won't be doing anything wrong. We've got backstage passes, after all – which means we're entitled to go anywhere.'

Seriously, I don't know where she gets her confidence from. If only she could bottle the stuff she'd make a fortune.

There was no time to discuss anything any further, as Mrs McCoy shouted up the stairs that we had to get a move on or they'd be late for the party, and we needed to be outside in the car in one minute or else.

Twenty minutes later, Mr McCoy pulled up outside the club. Mrs McCoy turned round in her seat to look at us.

'Right, so you've got your money for a taxi home?'

'Yes, Mum,' said Soph. Me and Abs nodded.

'And you'll make sure you get a licensed cab?'

'Yes, Mum,' said Soph. Me and Abs nodded again.

'And you're to be home no later than . . .'

'Half past ten!' we chorused.

'Right,' said Mrs McCoy, giving us all a beady look. 'And don't think I won't be ringing at ten thirty-one on the dot to check. Because I will.'

'Yes, Mum, I know. Um, Mum, have you seen the time?' Soph said innocently, just as her mother was opening her mouth to say something else. Mrs McCoy looked at her watch and gasped. 'Oh, no, we're going to be so late!' She turned to her husband and glared. 'Richard, why didn't you say something!'

We scrambled out of the car and Mr and Mrs McCoy drove off. I was still sure I was going to be sick, but Abs assured me that I couldn't possibly be sick as I'd hardly touched my burger, and as I hadn't eaten anything else since lunch, there would be nothing for me to actually throw up.

Holding out our tickets to be inspected by the bouncer, we made our way into the club. There were loads of people teeming around inside, waiting for Mirage to go on stage. I could feel the excitement in the air. It wasn't surprising. I'd read on the Internet earlier that due to the success of her last single, this was probably the last time Mirage would play a small venue like this. And as this was a secret gig, tickets hadn't gone on sale; they were only available through a competition on her fan club's site. I couldn't believe that I'd missed the competition – seriously, I live for stuff like that. But then, I guess I did have other things on my mind – like trying to help Mirage out of a huge hole.

We made our way to the backstage entrance, where a huge bouncer stood guard. I could feel the gaze of everyone in the place burning jealously into our backs. Some people were even whispering and pointing. The three of us couldn't help giggling and flicking our hair importantly.

There was a tense silence as the bouncer inspected our passes. I felt sure he was about to look up and say, 'What do you girls think you're playing at?' But he said nothing, just stood back to let us by. We headed into a dimly lit hallway. With a dart of shock I realised we were actually backstage. I silently hoped that we'd still be able to hear the music from here; it seemed a crime to be missing a Mirage concert, even in the name of Mystery!

'Right,' said Abs. 'I vote we start with the office.'

'Good plan,' said Soph. 'Er, where is it?'

'Here,' I said, opening a door and waving the girls inside.

'Er, Rosie?' said Abs, 'I think you'll find this is actually a broom cupboard.'

'Oh, right. My mistake,' I blushed.

'Well, it's got to be one of these,' said Soph, opening and closing a few doors and peering inside. 'Here it is,' she called. 'I've found it.'

Quickly checking that the coast was clear, we darted inside.

'OK,' said Abs, looking round the room with her hands on her hips. 'We know what we're looking for, right?'

'Yup,' me and Soph chorused. 'The missing CCTV footage.'

'What are you waiting for, then?' she said impatiently. 'Get looking!'

Honestly, I love Abs to death, but sometimes she is sooo bossy.

The three of us got to work. Abs started searching the desk, Soph looked in the bookcase and I tackled the filing cabinet, nodding my head to the beat pulsing through the walls.

Twenty minutes later, I sat back on my heels and sighed. 'This is hopeless. I've been through the whole of this filing cabinet from top to bottom, and all I've got to show for it is a load of paper cuts. It's not here.'

Soph looked up from the bookcase. 'It's not here either,' she said.

'Nor here,' said Abs, slamming shut the drawer of the desk irritably.

An awful thought struck me. 'What if it's just not here? What if the thief destroyed it, or threw it away?'

'Shhh!' said Abs.

'No,' I said kicking the filing cabinet with frustration. 'I won't shush! We've got to face it. The missing CCTV might be gone for good.'

'No, seriously, Rosie, shut up!' hissed Abs. 'I think someone's coming!'

The three of us froze. Sure enough, I could hear footsteps in the hallway outside. What's more, they were heading right towards us. Me, Abs and Soph looked at each other in horror.

'Hide!' mouthed Abs. The three of us dived for cover – Abs beneath the desk and me and Soph behind the curtains.

'I'm so glad these are floor-length,' Soph murmured, wiggling her eyebrows at me.

'I know!' I whispered back, fighting an urge to giggle hysterically.

We froze as the door opened and someone entered the room. There was a tiny hole in the curtains, right in front of me. Being careful not to move the material, I peered through the hole.

It was Simone. I held my breath as she walked over to the desk, where she suddenly stopped and looked down.

'Got you!' she said.

I looked at Soph in horror. Simone must have seen Abs! I swear, I felt my heart stop beating. As Simone reached down towards the desk, I closed my eyes, unable to look. Seconds later, I opened them again. I had to know the worst. I peered through the hole again. Simone was walking out of the office, jangling a set of keys in her hand. She hadn't seen Abs at all – she'd just been looking for her keys. I felt my knees practically buckle with relief.

'Has she gone?' hissed Soph.

Putting my finger to my lips, I carefully tiptoed to the door and listened. I could hear Simone's heels clicking further and further away.

'It's OK, guys,' I said. 'You can come out now. She's gone.'

Soph peered out cautiously from behind the curtains. 'That was close,' she said.

'Yeah, way too close,' I agreed. 'I reckon we should get out of here while the going's good.'

There was a scream from under the desk, then a sharp intake of breath. 'I don't believe it!' exclaimed Abs.

'What is it with you tonight, Abs?' I said, seriously annoyed this time. 'You're never normally this argumentative. I mean, can you even imagine what Simone would have done if she had found you underneath the desk? I'm putting my foot down. We are going to leave. Now.' I folded my arms, feeling immensely proud of myself for taking a stand.

'No, you idiot,' said Abs, poking her head out from under the desk and grinning at me. 'I mean, I don't believe what I've just found.'

Oh.

Me and Soph bent down and peered under the

desk. Abs was on her knees, a pulled-up floorboard next to her. 'I noticed it was loose when I was hiding,' she said, 'and it got me thinking that it might just be worth having a look underneath. And, it really, really was. Come and see!'

Me and Soph crawled towards her and peered into the gap where the floorboard had been.

'Yeuch!' Soph screamed. 'Dead mouse! Dead mouse!'

'I know!' said Abs. 'That made me scream too, but look next to it.'

Averting my eyes from the poor little dead mouse, I looked into the gap again. Beside the mouse was a stack of money. And beside that, covered in dust and what looked suspiciously like mouse poo, lay a DVD. Clearly marked across it were the words 'CCTV footage'.

Chapter Eight

Five minutes later, the three of us were heading back down the corridor, the DVD safely tucked inside Soph's over-sized pockets.

'See, not just fashion-forward – practical too,' Soph had winked as she slipped the DVD into her jeans. We'd left the cash where it was – we weren't in this for the money, after all. Besides, it would have been stealing.

'I vote we go straight home and watch the footage,' Abs said.

'Absolutely,' I agreed. Soph nodded too.

As we headed towards the backstage exit, I felt a giggle of relief rising in me. That had been close. I couldn't believe we'd got away with it so easily.

'Hey, you!' came a voice from behind me suddenly. 'Hold it right there!'

We whirled round and my heart sank. It was the minder who had escorted me out of Top Choonz and he was looking right at me. I stared at Abs and Soph in horror.

'I knew this was all too easy,' I hissed.

'Not so fast,' he said, walking towards me. 'You're not going anywhere –'

'You can't stop us,' interrupted Abs. 'We're totally entitled to be here. We've got passes. Look!' She waved her backstage pass in front of him.

'As I was saying,' the bouncer continued, as if Abs hadn't spoken, 'you're not going anywhere . . . without this.' He held out my denim jacket. 'You dropped it back there.' He nodded back down the corridor.

'Oh! Thank you. My jacket. Right. Thanks. Thank you,' I gabbled.

The bouncer looked at me as if I was a complete idiot. But I didn't even care. Linking arms with Abs and Soph, I headed through the exit, giggling with relief.

'What are *you* doing here?' came a disbelieving voice. I looked up to see Amanda Hawkins staring at us.

'Oh, nothing – just hanging out backstage.' I grinned at her, flashing my backstage pass under her nose. She stared at it, then back at me, her mouth hanging open in shock. You could practically see her brain working overtime, trying to figure out what was going on.

'Mirage invited us along when we were all having our nails done on Saturday,' I grinned.

Seeing her face after I said that had to be one of the best moments of my life. I mean, come on, how many times has she been horrible to me? Or Abs? Or Soph? Answer: approximately one billion times. And how often have I had the perfect put-down on my lips? Answer: never. Till now!

'Come on, girls, let's go,' I grinned at Abs and

Soph. The three of us high-fived and headed for the club's exit, leaving Amanda Hawkins completely lost for words. Probably for the first time ever!

We were still laughing about it when the taxi drew up outside Soph's house, twenty minutes later. 'Look at that,' Soph said, glancing at her watch. 'It's not even quarter to ten. No need to worry about Mum's curfew.'

'Put on the DVD, Soph,' said Abs, dumping her coat on the armchair and throwing herself on to the sofa.

'Yeah,' I said, snuggling back on to the sofa next to Abs. 'Hurry up, Soph.'

Soph stuck her head round the lounge door. 'I'm just making some snacks. After everything we've been through tonight, we're going to watch this DVD in style. Who's for hot chocolate?'

Abs and I groaned in unison, although I had to admit I was starting to feel a bit peckish. After all, I'd hardly touched my burger earlier, and lunch seemed a very, very long time ago.

Five minutes later, having brought in plates of cheese on toast plus bowls of crisps, Soph slipped the DVD into the machine. Standing up with the remote control in her hand, she turned to face me and Abs.

'Once there was a pop star called Mirage,' she said putting on her film-trailer voice. 'Beautiful and talented, it seemed like she had everything, but Mirage was hiding a secret that could destroy her. Only three schoolgirls could save her. Could they help her in time? Watch the movie to find out . . .'

'Get on with it!' me and Abs screamed, throwing cushions at her and giggling madly.

'OK, OK,' laughed Soph. 'Ladies, I give you . . . *CCTV*, the movie.'

Throwing herself on to the sofa between me and Abs, she pressed play.

I grabbed Soph and Ab's hands as the screen began to flicker. Just as we had suspected, it was the missing CCTV footage. But it showed far more than we had ever expected. We gasped in disbelief as the footage clearly showed the real thief placing money in Joe's jacket as it hung over the office chair. Not only that, the footage also showed the thief carefully moving the desk in the office and placing yet more money in the hiding place beneath the floorboards, before replacing the desk. A thief who, with her sleek, bobbed hair, designer suit and killer heels looked all too familiar . . .

'Simone!' we all said in unison, watching open-mouthed.

'Well, I knew she was evil,' said Abs, 'But I never thought she was *that* evil.'

'Oh, I did,' said Soph. 'You know, I wouldn't be surprised if she'd killed that poor little mouse, too.'

We all sat in silence for a moment, while the truth sank in. Simone was not only blackmailing Mirage – she'd set up Joe in the first place! Unbelievable!

'You know what?' said Abs, a grin starting to break out over her face. 'We've only gone and done it. We've got all the evidence we need to prove Joe's innocence.'

We all stared at each other. Then Soph started laughing and suddenly we were all on our feet, screaming and hugging each other.

'We've done it! We've really done it!' I shouted at the top of my lungs, jumping up and down on the sofa. 'Mirage is going to be totally psyched!'

It just didn't seem fair that she shouldn't hear straightaway. I looked at Soph's mobile lying on the table. Mine was upstairs and I couldn't be bothered to get it. Surely an innocent little text wouldn't hurt. Quickly I keyed in: GOT IT. E'THING'S GONNA B OK!

I jabbed in Mirage's number (yes, I *was* sad enough to have learnt it by heart – I mean, come on, who wouldn't if they had a pop star's number?) and pressed send before I could change my mind.

Abs and Soph were still holding each other and jumping up and down. Suddenly, Soph broke away and ran over to the DVD player. She pressed eject and, snatching up the DVD, kissed it. 'You, my beauty, are going with the rest of my precious belongings.'

Still laughing and shouting at the top of our voices we followed her upstairs as she headed for her bedroom. She kissed the DVD again and slid it under the pink fake-fur cover she'd made for her sewing machine.

'There,' she said. 'That's where I keep all my important stuff, like my design sketchbook. Now I know we won't lose it. Right,' she said, her brown eyes sparkling mischievously, 'I reckon we should call the gorgeous Joe and tell him the good news.'

'I don't know,' said Abs. 'Isn't it a bit late? It is a weeknight, after all.'

'This is the kind of news I can guarantee neither Mike nor Joe would mind being woken up for,' I said. 'Anyway, it's only just gone half-past ten.'

We headed downstairs again. Soph picked up the handset and dialled Mike's number. Joe answered the phone, and Soph put him on speakerphone. Between giggles of excitement we told him that we had footage that proved his innocence (and Simone's guilt) beyond a shadow of a doubt. For a minute there was complete silence.

'I . . . I . . . don't know what to say,' he stuttered. 'I just can't thank you enough. I don't believe it. Thank you. Thank you. Just wait till I tell Dad. I can't believe it. Thank you *so* much.'

We promised to bring the DVD round to his house the next day and put the phone down. Soph threw herself on to her back and kicked her legs in the air.

'I could think of plenty of ways he could thank me,' she giggled.

I slapped her leg. 'Soph! I've said it before and I'll say it again, he's eighteen. *Way* too old for you.'

'I know, I know! But a girl can dream, can't she?' She stretched her arms and yawned. 'I don't know about you two, but all this excitement has totally wiped me out. I say we clear up this mess, then head to bed.'

I suddenly realised how tired I was. 'Sounds good to me,' I said.

Abs nodded. 'I'm whacked,' she said.

Ten minutes later, everything had been put away, the rubbish had been thrown out and the three of us tripped up to bed. Soph was in her own bed and me and Abs were on blow-up mattresses on the floor.

The three of us chatted for a while, still giggling over the night's events, but we were all completely shattered and, one by one, we all fell asleep.

* * *

I don't know how long I'd been asleep when the sound of someone moving across the room woke me. I opened my eyes and sat up, blinking groggily as my eyes adjusted to the dark.

'Soph,' I whispered, 'is that you?'

'Guess again,' came a voice.

I gasped in fear; Simone Jones was standing over me.

Chapter Nine

I opened my mouth to scream, but before I could make a noise, Simone had grabbed my hair and dragged me out of bed. Reaching out with her other hand, she snapped on the bedroom light.

'Turn it off,' Abs groaned. 'I'm trying to sleep.'

'Sur-*prise*!' Simone smiled. 'One false move from you two, and this one . . .' she pulled me forward by my hair, '. . . could get seriously hurt.'

Abs and Soph scrambled up in bed, their eyes wide with horror.

'S-S-Simone? Wh-wh-what are you doing

here?' stammered Abs.

'Tut, tut, girls. Where are your manners? Aren't you going to offer me a drink?' she said. 'Actually, I'm not really in the mood for a drink. I feel more like watching a DVD. What do you think?' She turned to face me, tightening her grip on my hair. 'Got any interesting DVDs to watch?'

I decided to try and bluff it out.

'Um, I think Soph's got *High School Musical*. Ouch!' My eyes watered as Simone tightened her grip on my hair even more. She was incredibly strong – probably from all that time in the gym, keeping her figure perfect. 'Seriously, Simone, what are you doing here?'

'You know exactly why I'm here,' she snarled.

'No, honestly, we . . .' Abs tailed off lamely as Simone rolled her eyes and walked over to Soph's desk, dragging me behind her by my hair.

'Right, ladies,' she said. 'You've got a choice: we can do this the easy way and you can tell me exactly where the DVD is, or we can do it the difficult way – and I find it myself. And don't even *think* about trying to rescue your friend. I've got a black belt in karate and I'm not afraid to use it.'

Soph looked around desperately at the phone beside her bed.

'That won't work either,' Simone sneered. 'I've disconnected it, so you can't call for help.'

'Do your worst,' I said. 'We're not scared of you! Right, Abs? Right, Soph?'

'Right!' they echoed.

'Don't say I didn't warn you,' snapped Simone, pulling my hair so hard I thought it might actually come away from my scalp. Tears sprang to my eyes, but I didn't care. No way was I going to give in to Simone. No way. No sir. Not me. And no way was I about to let on how badly Simone was hurting me; Abs and Soph would cave straight away if they knew I was in any kind of real pain. Simone was too clever to get close enough for them to try and rescue me. Anyway, I was afraid of what might happen if they tried. Simone was as strong as a professional wrestler, even if she wasn't quite as bulgy with muscles.

Simone's eyes narrowed. 'Oh, you think you're all so smart, don't you? Well, you're not. You're not even smart enough to lock your own back door. How else do you think I got in here!'

Soph clapped her hand to her mouth, looking from me to Abs in horror. 'Oh, no,' she gasped. 'I must have forgotten to lock it before I went to bed, what with all the excitement and everything. Oh, guys, I'm so sorry!'

Abs reached out and hugged her. 'It doesn't matter, Soph. It's not your fault.'

'Ahhhh, how touching,' Simone smiled nastily. Still keeping a tight grip on my hair, she reached for Soph's schoolbag, which was sitting on the desk. She tipped it upside down so its contents spilled all over the floor.

'Hmmm, it's not in your bag I see,' she said. 'Never mind, still plenty of places to look.' And still only using one hand, she pulled open one of the desk drawers and started emptying the contents on to the carpet.

'I picked up the message you sent to Mirage

and it didn't take long to match the sender's number up with Sophie McCoy's fan-club membership. It was so good of you to register for text-message updates on Mirage. After that, it was easy to find out your address,' she boasted.

Soph stared at her, totally confused. 'What message? I didn't send Mirage any message!' she said. She looked at me and Abs. 'I swear I didn't.'

'Girls,' I whispered, 'it was me. I didn't think one little text message would hurt. I sent it from your phone, Soph – mine was upstairs and I couldn't be bothered to go and get it.' Tears welled up in my eyes. 'I'm so, so sorry.'

'It doesn't matter, Rosie, honestly,' said Abs, trying to smile, even though I could see her bottom lip trembling with fear. 'You weren't to know.'

'Oh, pur-*lease*. Someone pass the sick bag,' said Simone, moving on to Soph's chest of drawers. She started throwing clothes all over the carpet.

'Once I got here,' she continued, 'I was lucky enough to bump into one of your neighbours, Mrs Rumbles.'

'Oh, no, not Granny Grumbles,' muttered Soph. 'That old bat.'

'That old bat, as you call her, was a great help,' said Simone, still throwing clothes on to the floor. 'I've met her type before – nosy, irritable and a complete child-hater. Once I told her that I was here to complain to Mr and Mrs McCoy about their daughter, she was only too happy to stop for a little chat. She'd heard lots of laughing and screaming coming from your house earlier and thought you were having an all-night party. She'd wanted to complain to Mr and Mrs McCoy, but she knew they had gone out themselves. Imagine how happy I was to hear that?'

Having finished with the chest of drawers, Simone moved on to Soph's wardrobe, still managing to keep a tight grip on my hair.

'You might think you're smart, getting into the office and taking the DVD. But you didn't think it through. Once I get the DVD back, I'll go straight to the police and tell them that you broke into my office and stole money.'

'But we didn't take any money!' said Abs indignantly. 'We're not the thieves round here. You're the person who's been stealing, not us!'

'Ah, but the police won't know that. Especially when I show them the CCTV footage from this evening, which clearly shows you three taking something from the hiding-place in my office. Obviously I'll tell the police I didn't want to use the safe after Joe broke into it. After all, who's going to believe the word of three little thieves against me – a respected businesswoman.'

I closed my eyes. She was right. Why would the police believe us? The only people who knew what we were doing were Mike and Joe – and the police were hardly likely to listen to them, what with Joe already being accused of stealing from the club. We were in serious trouble.

I had a horrible thought. What if Mum believed her? What if she was totally disappointed and said she never wanted to see me again. And then I got sent to prison. And Mum never visited me cos she'd be too ashamed that a daughter of hers could have done such a thing. Then, years later, when I was finally let out of prison, I'd get married and have children and they'd never get to know their grandma. And one day my little daughter would come and sit on my knee and, putting her arms round my neck, say, 'Mummy, why does Granny Parker hate us?' and I'd have to choke back my tears and say, 'She doesn't hate us. She just . . .'

Simone pulled hard on my hair, snapping me back to the present.

OK, don't think about that, I told myself. *Just get through this.*

Simone kicked the chest of drawers in frustration. 'Right,' she said, 'I'm sick of this. I've given you every chance to tell me where the DVD is. No more Miss Nice Simone.'

She yanked my hair so hard that I fell to my knees, putting my hands to my head in pain. It felt as if a huge clump of hair had been ripped out.

Simone let out a cold laugh. 'Tell me where the DVD is or this one gets properly hurt,' she said, twisting her hand in my hair even more. I let out a yelp of pain.

'Stop it! Stop it!' sobbed Soph. 'I'll get you the DVD – just don't hurt Rosie.'

She jumped up from the bed.

'Don't, Soph, please don't,' I said, bursting into tears and closing my eyes to try and block out how much Simone was hurting me. 'Think of Mirage, think of Joe. The DVD's their only hope.'

'Soph's right,' said Abs, her voice shaking as she tried not to cry. 'You're the most important thing right now, Rosie. Soph, give her the DVD.'

Soph walked across the room towards the sewing machine. As she reached inside, found the disc and turned, DVD her hand, a pair of headlights lit up the room from a car turning into the driveway.

'Help!' I shouted at the top of my voice. 'HELP! HHHHHEEEELLLLLLPPPPPPPP!!!!'

'Richard! Richard!' came Mrs McCoy's familiar voice from outside the house. 'Something's going on with the girls.'

Simone froze. 'Give me the DVD,' she hissed.

'No *way*,' said Soph. 'Face it, Simone, the game's over. You lose.'

And she threw herself across the room and tackled Simone, who lost her balance and fell over backwards on top of me, knocking the wind right out of me. I started to cry again, not just cos I could hardly breathe, but because Simone had still been holding my hair and a huge clump of it had come right off in her hand. Plus Simone falling on top of me meant that my skirt had ridden right up, which meant my knickers were probably on show to the whole room.

The next thing I knew, the bedroom door burst open and Simone was lifted off me, much to my relief – for someone so skinny, that woman was seriously heavy. It must have been all those muscles. I was crying my head off like a baby. I'm not joking. I was bawling the way Soph did the day she read in *Vogue* that grey was the new black – the day after she'd dyed her whole wardrobe black.

Then Mrs McCoy was there and she put her

arm around me, while I hiccupped and snivelled into her jumper. And Abs and Soph came rushing over and we all hugged each other.

A few minutes later, Mr McCoy walked back into the bedroom. He was out of breath and very pink in the face. 'I've locked that mad woman in the dining room,' he said. 'Boy, for a tiny slip of a thing, she can sure put up a fight.' He wiped his forehead with a hankie. 'Mr Henderson from next door heard the racket we were making. He's standing guard until the police get here.'

He fixed us with a serious stare. 'Right, you three, I think you've got some serious explaining to do.'

Chapter Ten

Me, Abs and Soph sat on the sofa in the lounge while Mrs McCoy fussed around us, fetching blankets and hot, sweet tea. It turned out that Mrs McCoy had tried to ring at ten-thirty like she'd said she would, but the phone went straight to the answering service. While Mr McCoy had tried to reassure her that it meant Soph was probably on the phone ordering pizza or something, Mrs McCoy had had a bad feeling in the pit of her stomach. Later on, she'd tried Sophie's mobile, but no one answered. We hadn't even heard it ring, we'd been so scared by Simone. And in the end she'd made Mr McCoy leave the party and drive her home, so she could see everything was OK with her own eyes. Boy, was I glad she had!

'Are you feeling a little better, Rosie?' she asked, pushing my hair away from my eyes.

'Yes, thank you, Mrs McCoy,' I said in a weak voice. You know, the type of voice you use when you're pretending to be sick. Although Mrs McCoy had told Mr McCoy that explanations could wait for now, as we were obviously in shock, I still wasn't sure how much trouble we were all in. And even though Mr McCoy had been distracted by Simone throwing herself repeatedly against the dining-room door in an attempt to escape, and both he and Mr Henderson were now having to lean on the door to stop her from getting out, it was obvious from the way a vein was popping in his forehead that he *really* wasn't happy.

A few minutes later, the police arrived. Simone was released from the dining room and led out of the house. I could see through the lounge windows a policeman was trying to get her into the police car. Simone was obviously refusing to get in and had knocked the policeman's cap on to the ground. I watched as he calmly picked her up and physically put her in the car. All the neighbours who had come out of their own houses to have a good gawk applauded. The policeman picked up his cap and took a little bow.

A policeman and policewoman had stayed behind to take down our version of events. We told the story from beginning to end, over and over again. And again. And again. I'd practically lost my voice by the time the policeman finally nodded at the policewoman, who closed her notebook.

By the look on the policeman's face, it was clear that he wasn't impressed by our story.

The conversation went something like this:

Policeman: *Right, so it didn't occur to you to go to the police?*
Abs: *Um, no.*

Policeman: *So, basically, you're saying that you thought three schoolgirls could make a better job of helping Miss Mullins, who was being blackmailed, than the police. Who, may I add, are highly trained in such matters.*
Me: *Um, well, when you put it like that . . .*
Policeman: *And at no point did it cross any of your minds when you were searching Miss Jones's office at the club that you were trespassing and if you had been caught you could have been in serious trouble, not just with Miss Jones but with the police?*
Soph: *Well, er . . . no. We were just trying to help Mirage.*
Policeman: *And it never struck you that you were dealing with a serious criminal who would probably be prepared to go to any lengths to make sure they weren't caught?*
Abs, me and Soph start to cry.

Mr McCoy stood up at that point. 'While I am also surprised at the girls,' he said, 'I think they have probably been through enough tonight and need to get some rest. I will make sure that all three of them understand the seriousness of this matter.'

The policeman and policewoman got up to leave. As they reached the lounge door, the policeman turned round and winked at us.

'By the way, if any of you three young ladies fancy going into the force when you leave school, you'll be only too welcome,' he said. 'Good detectives are always needed.'

He thanked Mr and Mrs McCoy and left. Me, Abs and Soph looked at each other and rolled our eyes. I mean, come on, *police officers*? What the crusty old grandads? Everyone knows that I want to be a serious novelist and write the next *Pride and Prejudice* or *Harry Potter* or something. Soph, of course, is going to be a fashion designer, while Abs – well, Abs is so smart, she'll probably be in charge of the world or something.

* * *

The next morning, I was at home in my PJs and dressing gown. Mum had collected me from Soph's earlier. She'd been totally shocked by what had happened and had pretty much lectured me all the way home. But once we got indoors, she ran me a hot bath and told me we were both going to play hooky for the day. Nan, on the other hand, was in a right old mood. Not because her only granddaughter had had her life practically threatened by a criminal, and by doing so had got herself into trouble with the police. Oh, no. She couldn't believe that a *real* crime had been committed right under her nose and she didn't have a clue. Honestly, whatever happened to grey-haired old grandmothers who sit in rocking chairs and knit jumpers? That's what I want to know.

Anyway, I was sitting in the kitchen munching some toast and reading my fave magazine, *Star Secrets*, when the doorbell went. Mum went to answer it. Two minutes later she was back. 'Um, Rosie, there's a visitor for you.' She stepped aside and I nearly fell off my stool in shock. Mirage Mullins, large as life, was standing in my kitchen. I kid you not.

'Hi, Rosie,' she said. 'I just wanted to let you know that the police have dropped all charges against Joe. I wanted to thank you. If it wasn't for you and the others – well, I dread to think what would have happened to Joe. And to me.'

And suddenly she came running towards me and gave me the biggest hug, like, ever. I hugged her right back.

'Listen,' she said, pulling back. 'I'm playing at a special police fundraiser on Saturday night. I'd like you, Sophie and Abs to be my backing singers. What do you say?'

'Ye-ye-yesss!' *Hang on a minute. That was weird.* My voice didn't even sound like mine. In fact, it sounded a lot like Mum. As I whipped round, Mum put her hand – the same hand that had just punched the air – over her mouth.

'Sorry,' she said. 'It's just the thought of my little girl on stage. *Singing*!'

* * *

That Saturday, me and Abs and Soph stood backstage with Mirage and Joe. Mirage's face was pink with happiness and she was clinging on to Joe as if he might disappear in a puff of smoke. He gave me a shy little smile and I beamed happily back.

'Good luck, girls,' he said. 'I'm going to go out front and watch the show. See you when you get off stage.'

'Ready?' Mirage asked, smiling at us.

'Uh-huh,' we grinned.

'Oh, and Soph,' said Mirage, 'don't forget you're just miming.'

I bit back a giggle. Soph's singing voice is sooo bad, Mirage had taken one listen and told her to mime. To make up for it, though, she had said Soph could design all our stage costumes. And it had to be said, Soph had totally outdone herself. We were all dressed in gorgeous pink off-the-shoulder sequinned tops over cropped black trousers that had pink ribbon sewn along the bottom hems.

'I know, I know,' said Soph. 'What can I say? My mum says calling me tone-deaf is an insult to all tone-deaf people.'

Laughing, Mirage stepped out on to the stage. The crowd went wild.

Mirage held her hands up and started to speak. 'Thank you all for coming,' she said. 'I'd like you to welcome on to the stage three girls who are not just fantastic backing singers. If it wasn't for them, I wouldn't be here tonight. Abs, Soph, Rosie, come on out.'

As we stepped on to the stage and launched into the first song, I could see practically the whole of our school – who Mirage had invited to see us perform – jumping up and down in excitement. The rest of the cast from the school play were practically going crazy, whistling and cheering. All apart from Amanda Hawkins, who was in the front row, slack-jawed with disbelief. Some of the teachers had turned up too. I could see Madame Bertillon humming along, next to Mr Adams. And Time Lord seemed to have totally forgotten all his lectures on how we shouldn't be impressed by celebrity and was standing right in front of the stage, shouting, 'Miss Mullins? Miss Mullins? We should get together after the show. I'm a fellow celebrity too. In fact, you might recognise me. I was in the original *Doctor Who*. I've just written a musical which I'd love to show you!' I grinned at Abs and Soph, who winked back at me. As the first song ended, the audience went wild. Mirage turned round and gave me a huge smile. 'Thank you,' she mouthed.

You know what? Having a talent for trouble seriously rocks sometimes!

Megastar

Everyone has blushing blunders – here are some from your Megastar Mysteries friends!

Mirage

I was on stage at a pop concert, singing and dancing to my latest top tune. The audience were going wild, and I thought it was for my awesome singing. Then my backing singer started making all these weird arm movements at me. I thought she'd come up with a new dance routine, but then I realised that she was trying to get my attention. I'd somehow managed to twist my microphone round myself and hitch my skirt up, flashing my pants to the whole crowd! I went redder than a raspberry!

Rosie

I was after a new CD player for my birthday, so Mum and I headed into town. We finally found some that I liked, so I started playing with them and seeing which one would look coolest in my room. Then I heard this really, really loud singing coming from somewhere. I turned round and there was Mum, belting out a Bananarama tune, flailing her arms around like a mad lady. Everyone in the shop was staring at her in disbelief. I wished the ground would open up and swallow me! Yikes!

Cringes

Soph

We were making our own T-shirts in art and I had such an awesome idea for mine that I couldn't wait to get to school (which is très unusual for me!). So, I grabbed a bagel, ran out of the house and headed to school. What I didn't know was that I was in such a hurry that I still had my pyjama top on and I was wearing one slipper and one school shoe! It was sooo not a good look!

Soph and Rosie were round at mine for a sleepover and we were busy playing truth or dare, which was très interesting! After we'd all spilled the beans about our crushes, we scoffed a midnight feast and fell asleep. The next morning I woke up to find Megan had scrawled 'Abbie loves Mr Adams' all over my schoolbooks! She'd been listening in to us all night and I had to play with her dolls for a week just to get her to shut up! Grrr!

Have You Got

Try our quiz to see if you could be the next Mirage!

1. You spend your Saturdays . . .

a. At your stage school/singing lessons

b. Hitting the shops

c. Hanging out with your mates

2. When you go to school discos, you . . .

a. Hog the stage and show the whole school all your latest moves

b. Make up some funky dance routines

c. Hide in the toilets having a gossip

3. You dream of winning . . .

a. A BRIT award

b. An Oscar

c. Anything!

4. At sleepovers you're the one who . . .

a. Gets on the karaoke and doesn't let anyone else near it

b. Gives everyone makeovers

c. Ends up doing lots of dares

Pop Potential?

5. What would you give up to be famous?

a. Everything, you're so going to be a star

b. Ummm, chocolate?

c. Nothing, you don't need fame that badly!

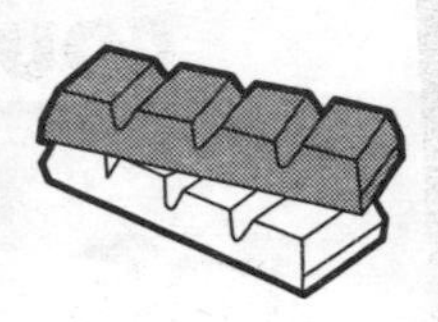

6. You don't leave the house without your . . .

a. Huuuge, celeb-style sunglasses

b. Posse of mates

c. Purse

Mostly As: Pop Princess

You're a Mirage in the making! You're always singing, forever copying your fave stars and ready to take the pop world by storm!

Mostly Bs: Pop Performer

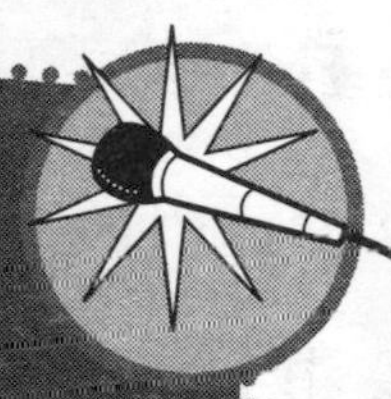

Hmmm, you like pop but it doesn't rule your life. You're just as happy shopping, being with your mates and just having as much fun as possible!

Mostly Cs: Pop Off

Pop's not really that important to you and you'd much rather be with your mates than be famous and have a life of total luxury . . .

Soph's Customising Cool

Check out Soph's top tips for a pop-tastic T-shirt!

What you need:

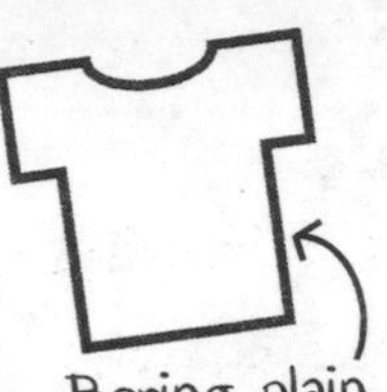

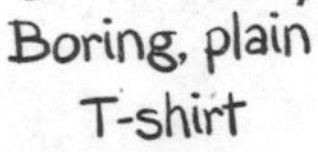

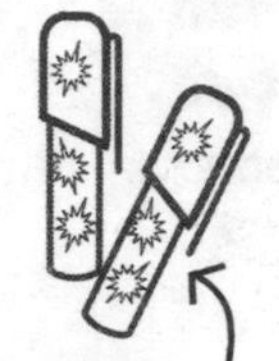

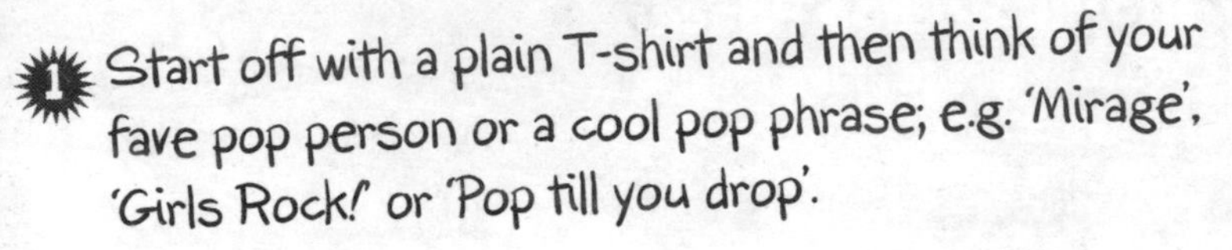

1. Start off with a plain T-shirt and then think of your fave pop person or a cool pop phrase; e.g. 'Mirage', 'Girls Rock!' or 'Pop till you drop'.

2. Grab some scrap paper and practise writing your phrase on it, using the glitter pens. Make your writing large and really funky!

3. Once you're happy with what you're writing, go ahead and write it on your T-shirt. Now glam it up by gluing on some sequins and making it look totally rockin'!

Fact File

Fact File

NAME: Rosie Parker (although some people prefer to call her Nosy Parker!)

AGE: 14

STAR SIGN: Sagittarius

HAIR: Long and blonde

EYES: Blue

LOVES: Finding out everything there is to know about pretty much everyone

HATES: Spending more than five seconds in the company of Amanda Hawkins

LAST SEEN: Sitting on the floor of the newsagent, surrounded by all the latest celeb magazines

MOST LIKELY TO SAY: 'What's the plan, Stan?'

WORST CRINGE EVER: Her mum turning up at parents evening straight from a Banana Splits gig and dressed in cropped dungarees, a checked shirt and pink leggings! Oh, the shame!

1 Grab a blank piece of paper and write your mobile phone number on it.

2 Now add up all the numbers in your mobile number and keep on adding them up till you end up with just one number.

3 Once you have the final number, read on to see what it says about you!

Don't forget to work out all your mates' numbers, too, and if you don't have a mobile just use your home phone number!

Find out what YOUR phone number says about YOU!

1 You're always happy, super-generous and love spending time looking after your fave people!

2 You can be a bit shy but you're also totally loyal and one of the best secret-keepers ever!

3 You love to take charge and you're a perfect party planner, no wonder you have sooo many mates!

4 You're a real daring diva and you'll have a go at anything. You're also great at making sleepovers special!

5 You're always on the go and your mates struggle to keep up! You're also mega brainy and very confident!

6 You're a class clown and love making people giggle. You're also a chilled chick who hates arguing!

7 You're animal mad and love anything cute! You're fab at solving problems and great at giving advice!

8 You're full of energy and never get bored. You love sports and always get everyone involved!

9 You're mega creative and you're always doodling. You're also the queen of gossip and never stop talking!

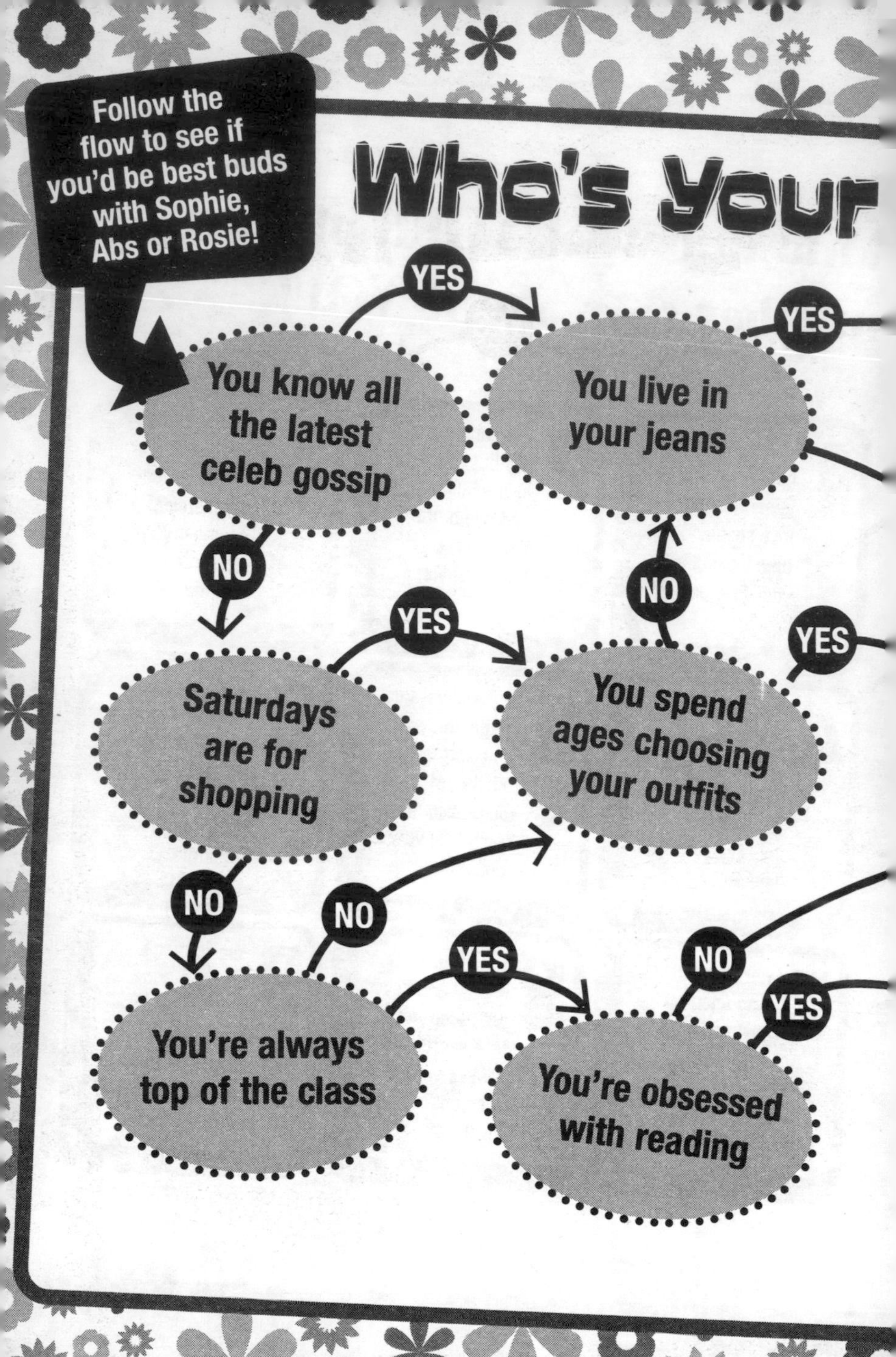
Follow the flow to see if you'd be best buds with Sophie, Abs or Rosie!
Who's Your
YES
YES
You know all the latest celeb gossip
You live in your jeans
NO
NO
YES
YES
Saturdays are for shopping
You spend ages choosing your outfits
NO
NO
YES
NO
YES
You're always top of the class
You're obsessed with reading

Megastar Mate?

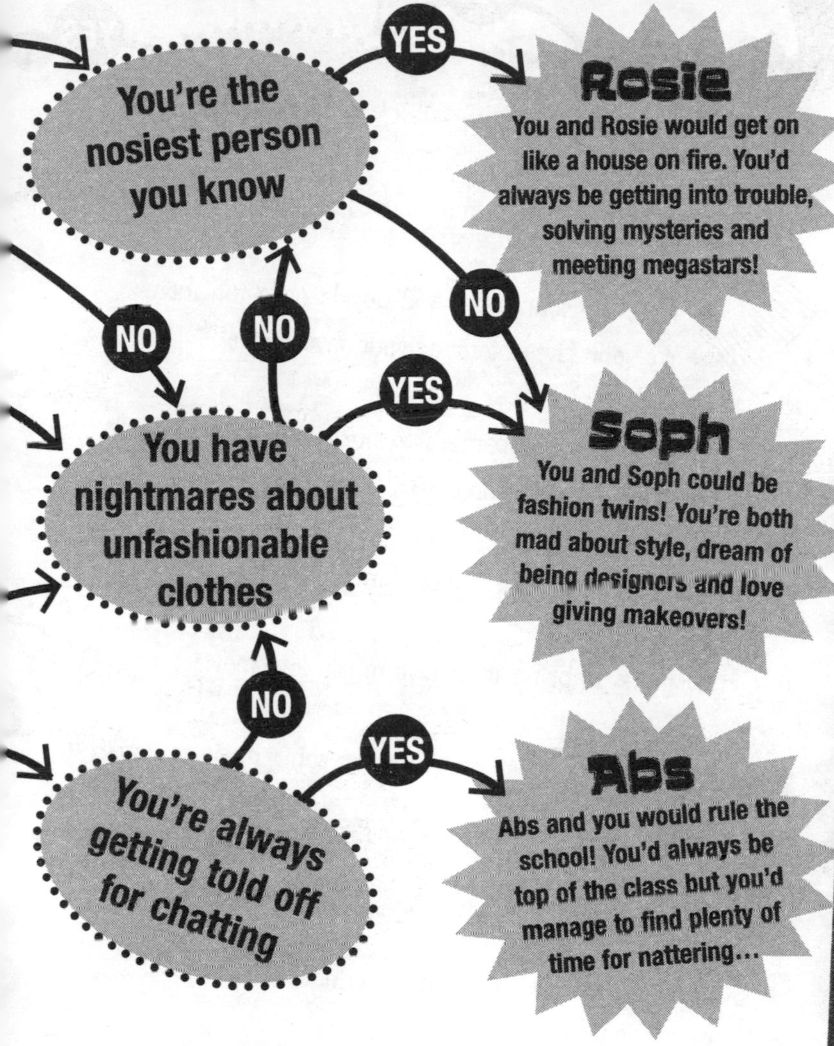

You're the nosiest person you know

YES

NO

Rosie

You and Rosie would get on like a house on fire. You'd always be getting into trouble, solving mysteries and meeting megastars!

NO

NO

You have nightmares about unfashionable clothes

YES

Soph

You and Soph could be fashion twins! You're both mad about style, dream of being designers and love giving makeovers!

NO

You're always getting told off for chatting

YES

Abs

Abs and you would rule the school! You'd always be top of the class but you'd manage to find plenty of time for nattering...

The Best Sleepover,

Sleepover essentials:

★ Invite your best mates – they know how to really have fun!

★ Make some yummy food – think choccies, mini pizzas and popcorn!

★ Decorate your room and decide on a fun theme, ike your fave colour or your fave movie!

★ Clear away anything embarrassing (including your old dolls and any dodgy fashion choices!)

★ Make space for practising your dance moves!

★ Get everyone to bring their fave music and movies!

★ Each have make-up at the ready for some mega makeovers!

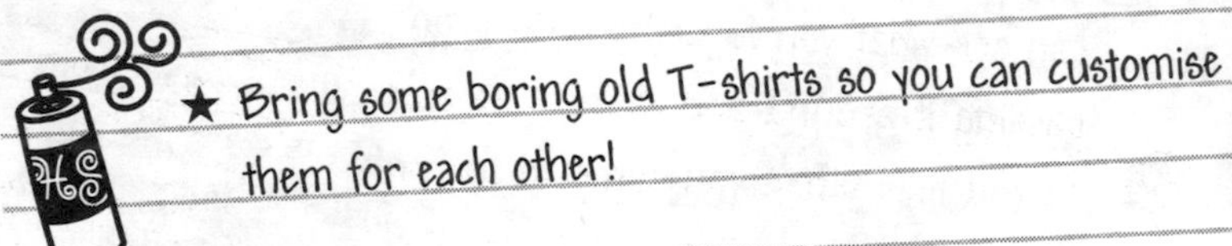

★ Bring some boring old T-shirts so you can customise them for each other!

★ Start off by revealing your biggest cringes to get everyone giggling!

Ever! Read on for how to make your sleepover really rock!

Great games:

Get some sticky notes and write a different famous person on each one. Turn them over and take it in turns to pick one up and stick it on your forehead. Make sure you can't see who it is. Then ask each other yes and no questions to find out who you are. The winner is the first person to guess correctly!

BRITNEY

Give everyone some pieces of paper and get them to write down five truth questions and five dares. Now make a pile of truth questions and a pile of dares and shuffle them up. Take it in turns to work through the truths and dares and see how much fun you have!

TRUTH
DARE

Using an A4 piece of paper, take it in turns to write one line of a story and then fold the paper over so no one can see what you've written. Keep on passing it around and make it as silly as you like. When you come to the end of the paper read it out and see how mad it is!

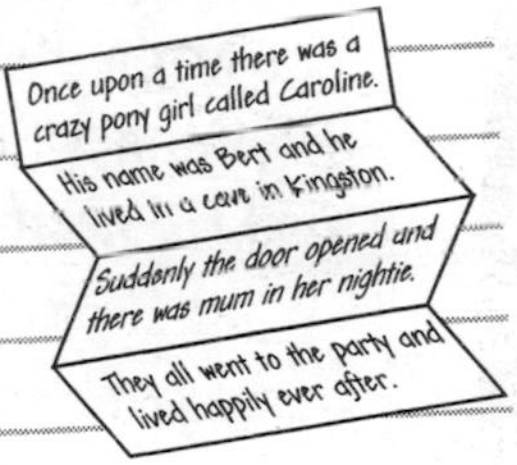

Once upon a time there was a crazy pony girl called Caroline.
His name was Bert and he lived in a cave in Kingston.
Suddenly the door opened and there was mum in her nightie.
They all went to the party and lived happily ever after.

Pam's Problem Page

Never fear, Pam's here to sort you out!

Dear Pam,

I've got a nightmare manager who is blackmailing me and causing me lots of stress! What can I do to get away from her and enjoy my life again?

Mirage

Pam says: *Oooh, now that's a bit of a tricky one, dear. Are you sure she's blackmailing you? Maybe you've been watching too much Miss Marple and you've got a bit confused. I saw one episode where this man thought a lady was trying to kill him when she was only really trying to borrow his umbrella! I'm sure that your manager is really a very nice lady and you just need to have a chat with her and get it all sorted out. Why don't you sit down together with a pack of custard creams? I'm sure you'll be friends again in no time!*

Can't wait for the next
book in the series?
Here's a sneak preview of

Fusion

Chapter One

I couldn't believe we were going on holiday to Smallhampton. For a *fortnight*. I mean, it was bad enough when Abs and Soph were both away at half-term, but at least that was only for a week. Now I had to cope for two weeks without them! In a *holiday park*. Me, Rosie Parker, friend to the stars – well, OK, one star – in a holiday park! Quelle horreur!

I was stunned when Mum told me where we were going.

'It'll be fun, Rosie,' she said, coming into my

room with an armload of washing. 'I chose a really great place. It's got a disco and everything.' Then she started giggling for some reason.

I just looked at her like she was a mad woman. Then it clicked. *Oh, no. Knowing Mum, she's probably booked the one holiday park that only has eighties music for entertainment. Nightmare*!

'Mum, for the last time, I do not want to dance to Wham! with you!' I said, rolling my eyes.

'Now *that* was a great band,' she said, smiling wistfully as she left the room.

I thought about what she'd said. She was right – there could be some cute boys there. That would make up for two weeks in the middle of nowhere, away from my best friends.

Yeah, well, that's what I thought . . . until Soph invited me and Abs to stay with her in France! Soph's family are mega-rich – well, richer than me and Mum and Nan, anyway – and they were hiring a really big villa near the coast, with a pool. Soph said it was like one of those places you see on *MTV Cribs*, with really large rooms and flowers everywhere, and a pool table and a fully stocked fridge (which you know the celeb never touches, because they're on some crazy diet or something, and they've got a personal chef anyway). I was *so* desperate to go. We would get a tan for a start, and there would be French boys there. I could practise my Français: 'Bonjour! Une baguette, s'il vous plaît.' You see, I'm a natural!

That day, Soph and Abs and I spent all of French class getting the phrase 'un beau garçon' into every conversation, which really annoyed Madame Bertillon:

> ***Soph:*** *Bonjour. Je voudrais un beau garçon, s'il vous plaît.*
> ***Moi:*** *Oui, oui. Nous avons deux garçons ici . . .*
> ***Madame Bertillon*** *(in that sort of growly bark she does): Girls! You're supposed to be in a bakery!*
> ***Amanda Hawkins*** *(my arch-enemy): Yeah,* duh.

We had brilliant plans. We'd even decided to colour-coordinate our bikinis and nail varnish. OK, Soph had decided that. But then Mum went and put a dampener on the whole thing.

'But Rosie, I've already booked the holiday park for those weeks,' she said. 'I can't cancel it now. I'm sorry, love, but you can't go to France.'

I couldn't believe it. She was spoiling everything. 'But Mum . . .'

'I'm sorry, Rosie. But I'm not going to ruin our family holiday just because you and your friends want to swan off together. You see enough of them as it is. I'm sure you'll survive for two weeks without them.'

TWO WEEKS ALONE! I'D BE A SOCIAL OUTCAST!

We had an emergency meeting at Abs's house.

'Did you try flattery?' suggested Abs helpfully. 'Y'know, like she might meet a nice man without you cramping her style?'

'Yep.'

'Did you try bribery?' asked Soph.

'And sulking and shouting and all that. But I still have to go.' I sighed. 'I can't believe you two are going to be in France without me.'

We all sighed.

For the next three weeks, Abs and Soph were really brilliant. They managed not to talk about it in front of me, but I could tell they were really excited about the sun, and the pool, and the French boys . . .

They came round to say goodbye the day we left. Soph had brought some nail varnish with her, to decorate my wellies. They looked *quite cool* once she'd finished, actually, even though I wouldn't have chosen blue frogs myself. That's Soph for you. Always ahead of the fashion game.

'You laugh now, my friend,' she said, 'but you wait. In a few months' time, customised wellies will be in all the fashion mags. Just think of all those celebs who go to festivals. What do they wear? Wellies!'

'Yeah, but blue frogs?' I said.

'Hey, you will text us the whole time, won't

you?' said Abs, changing the subject. 'And we'll have broadband at the villa, so we can instant message each other, too.'

'Bien sûr, ma soeur. *If* there's a computer. I'll be so bored, I'll be bothering you, like, every hour. In fact, I'll be so bored I might even look at that play we're supposed to read for drama. I've packed it, just in case.'

'Wow!' Soph was impressed. 'Mr Lord will love you. Maybe he'll make you the lead in the play next term.'

'Yeah, right,' I said. 'Like Time Lord will *ever* spot my star potential.'

'Rosie!' Nan called up the stairs. 'Time to go!'

I sighed, rolled my eyes and trudged out of my room. Abs and Soph trailed behind me, both doing a very good job of looking sad.

Nan was waiting in the hall. 'Have fun, girls!' she trilled to Abs and Soph. 'Don't go doing anything I wouldn't do!'

'Like what?' they asked.

This was normally the cue for Nan to start

warning them about strange men or over-friendly new neighbours who could be up to no good, but we were saved by a shout from Mum. She was in the sitting room, where she was trying to sort out the satellite TV.

'I think it's broken!' she called.

'What?!' Nan was horrified. She trotted into the sitting room to check out the awful truth. 'It can't be! What about the *Murder Mystery Weekend* special? I won't be able to record it!'

I could sympathise with Nan. We were both being torn from the things (or people) we loved – in my case, the girls and my whole life; in her case, the TV with its many, many, *many* murder-mystery shows. Nan loves them. Particularly *Murder, She Wrote*. Angela Lansbury – the actress who plays Jessica Fletcher, the writer–detective – is her favourite. I don't know why. Personally, I think it's really dodgy that a murder happens wherever Jessica goes. But Nan thinks she's brilliant. 'Watch and learn, Rosie, watch and learn,' she says. It's amazing I ever get to watch *EastEnders* or *Big*

Brother, or anything, really, considering how she hogs the TV.

Anyway, Mum had decided we all did too much telly-watching. Although there would be a TV at this park, she was planning to limit how much we could watch. 'We should be getting out there and meeting people,' she said, 'not getting square eyes in front of the telly.'

Nan was not happy. Especially because the *Murder Mystery Weekend* special started right when we were supposed to be driving to this holiday park. The Satellite TV was her new toy and her lifeline.

'I'm sorry, Mother, but I can't work this blooming thing out,' Mum said. 'Rosie, you're better at it than I am. Come and fix it, please. But remember we have to leave in ten minutes.'

'Er, Rosie, we've gotta go,' said Soph. 'Soz.'

'We'll call you,' said Abs. 'Promise.'

I grabbed them and hugged them close. It was going to be a *long* two weeks. Then, sighing again, I trudged into the sitting room. Even my dramatic parting from Soph and Abs had been ruined.

* * *

Just a few hours later, I was feeling like I'd been travelling to Smallhampton for my whole *life*. It didn't help that my mum insisted on playing Bananarama songs most of the way. Like, who even cares about them now? Mum, that's who. She warbled along to their track 'Robert De Niro's Waiting' as she sped round a roundabout, making me and Nan lurch sideways.

'*Mum!*' I pleaded.

'Oh, sorry, Rosie. How about we put something of yours on instead? Something by that Mirage Muggins? Is that better? More trendy?'

Honestly. I wonder about her sanity sometimes. What hope do I have? Especially when you consider I'm related to Nan, too, who spent the whole car journey muttering about the satellite TV. Thank goodness for mobiles. I spent most of the journey texting things like 'Help!' and 'got 2 get outta here' to Soph and Abs. And compiling this list:

Top ten reasons why going on holiday with my family is really annoying:

1. The music in the car. For every Mirage Mullins song I'm allowed to play, we have to have an eighties 'classic'. Oh, what I'd do for an MP3 player . . .
2. Stopping for a wee and a cup of tea every few miles. Nan loves checking out every service-station toilet and how clean it is. Plus, she can't cope without a cuppa for very long. I have tried to point out that I can't cope without an injection of cash for very long, but Mum has failed to get the hint.
3. At this holiday park, I will be stuck in the middle of nowhere, with no friends and no shops. Aaargh!
4. I'll probably be forced to take part in organised activities like crazy golf . . . or darts . . . or dance classes. Actually, if the dance classes get you to dance like the celebs on *Strictly Come Dancing*, that would be cool.

Apart from the spangly shirts they make the men wear. But I bet this place will have eighties dance classes, where you wear really gross leotards and legwarmers. Mum's idea of heaven!

5. I'm sooo not going to meet anyone famous there.
6. I know Abs and Soph will have loads of fun without me. And meet sexy French boys.
7. I may be so bored I have to do some homework.
8. I have to put up with Nan moaning about missing the *Murder Mystery Weekend* special.
9. There probably won't be anyone my age there, and I'll be forced to make friends with old ladies and young boys who are in the Scouts.
10. It's for a whole *fortnight*!

So, basically, by the time we got to the holiday park, we were all a bit miserable. Mum was trying to be in a good mood, but even she had been ground down by Nan's muttering, and my heavy, dramatic sighs.

It was getting dark as we pulled in through the gates, down the track that took us to reception. I could see lots of lodges that were supposed to look like log cabins. They all had cars next to them. It seemed to be a popular place. I just hoped it was popular with cool people.

Mum went into reception to say we'd arrived, and while Nan went to find a toilet, I wandered through to the restaurant area. The yellow plastic chairs and laminated tables that were fixed to the ground reminded me of the school canteen. I shuddered.

Then I caught sight of a poster on the wall. It listed the entertainment for the week, so I went over for a closer look. *Best to get the bad news over with in one go.*

To my surprise, it actually looked quite cool. There was some band called Fusion playing all fortnight, and they looked really good from the photo! The girls were wearing funky clothes, and one of the boys was seriously cute. He had a guitar slung round his neck, and was holding a microphone, looking really cool. He had dark wavy hair and piercing blue eyes. I know it sounds weird, but I felt like he was staring back at me as I stood gazing at the poster.

Fusion. It sounded a bit familiar. Maybe I'd read something about them somewhere? It said they were 'up-and-coming' on the poster. Wouldn't it be cool if I saw them play just before they shot to mega-fame?!

'Rosie? Rosie! Oh, there you are!' said Mum, coming in to the 'restaurant'. 'Come on, I've got the keys. We're in number forty-two. Where's your nan?'

'Loo,' I said automatically, as I followed Mum out. With a hot band like Fusion hanging around the place, maybe this holiday was going to be a tiny bit interesting after all . . .